T0156713

BETTER

THAN

SEX

CAKE

Sarah Wilson

iUniverse, Inc.
New York Bloomington

Better Than Sex Cake

Copyright © 2009 by Sarah Wilson

All rights reserved. No part of this book may be used or reproduced by any means, graphic, electronic, or mechanical, including photocopying, recording, taping or by any information storage retrieval system without the written permission of the publisher except in the case of brief quotations embodied in critical articles and reviews.

This is a work of fiction. The characters, entities, incidents, and dialogues are the product of the author's imagination. Any similarity to actual events, entities, or persons (living or dead) is coincidental and not intended by the author. Although some real celebrities and locations may be mentioned, all are used fictitiously.

iUniverse books may be ordered through booksellers or by contacting:

iUniverse
1663 Liberty Drive
Bloomington, IN 47403
www.iuniverse.com
1-800-Authors (1-800-288-4677)

Because of the dynamic nature of the Internet, any Web addresses or links contained in this book may have changed since publication and may no longer be valid. The views expressed in this work are solely those of the author and do not necessarily reflect the views of the publisher, and the publisher hereby disclaims any responsibility for them.

ISBN: 978-1-4401-1857-9 (pbk)
ISBN: 978-1-4401-1874-6 (cloth)
ISBN: 978-1-4401-1858-6 (ebk)

Printed in the United States of America

iUniverse rev. date: 1/16/2009

I Dedicate This Book -

To my wonderful family and friends that have supported

me in my writing endeavors...

Sarah Wilson

PROLOGUE

Some people were simply born in the wrong place. The first thing such individuals searched for was a map, which Betty Babbs had always referred to as her wish book, and the second was a ticket out. Life to her in the mountains was a prison stretch, which had dutifully been served by applying herself to schoolwork. She'd been ready to leave Franklin since she was a toddler, and finally managed her escape - which arrived in the form of a journalism scholarship to Western Carolina. For side money she'd supported herself throughout school with a bakery job. Little did her family know she would become infamous for her "Better Than Sex Cake" recipe.

Her parents were hesitant with her decision to travel two counties over where people bonded to dishonesty and depravity. They assumed this conclusion because of all the troubles spelled out on television. In the end she won the conflict using a strategy that included equal amounts of unrelenting promises, and insistent tears. Betty constantly reminded them that amid the scenic beauty of their present landscape a scar of abandoned houses and junkyard trailers existed due to Appalachian poverty, including a description of how community stores mainly sold an impoverished diet of biscuits and pizza. Everywhere you looked the kind faces of these gentle people wore weariness and an uneasiness that comes from years of looking over their shoulders. She had to escape this future. Being amenable and kind was not her objective. Her mother was impressionable and good-natured; Betty was often pigheaded and blinkered, the sort of girl who went barefoot in spite of all warnings to watch out for snakes.

Babbs was a collected work, yellowed with frail edges and broken in places, bent at the corners precariously held together. She couldn't call herself complete, and lived in washed out letters that even her family didn't recognize. Her pages unglued and jumbled in haphazard order often landed in disarray. She wanted to be more than a story written in the dark of night, poetry captured by starlight and hold onto the ability to float on dreams. The only recipe she really longed for was to find love, a successful job, never becoming that book left in the corner gathering dust. Betty had hidden long enough from the sun under the arms of loving parents. For the first time in her life she was in charge of her life. Betty landed heels down and running in the county of Stanly, North Carolina.

Norwood was an unfamiliar town, and it bloomed pink across her new geography, the piedmont area of North Carolina. Sprawled between two rivers Lake Tillery appeared manicured and quiet. A town of tiny steeples rose from the blue-sky sanctuary. Rolling landscape that she was born to climb and escape forward in her life spread out before her. At that moment Babbs knew the area and herself both had an eye for the sun, and for what makes men weak-kneed; the slow start, the rise up hard, the fall down easy. Then the silence that makes one want to put an arm to a hip, to hold that crippled pause of daylight.

It was her heart that subconsciously spoke to her telling her she was meant to be there. A small town filled with gently dusted light and one she could learn to appreciate. This would be where her binding would be restored, and her spine reinforced. Her patina would be replenished to a polish of fine leather and a life worth reading about.

1 - A NEW LIFE

At a quarter past midnight she set her wallpaper pan next to the toilet, the paper in the tub, her bathroom the newest butt in a wedge of odd-hour repairs.

Betty's antique mahogany dresser, with a mirror attached to it, one that could be tilted back and forth held photos that were sun-faded and curled with age. A toothy, blonde-haired girl in her teens, with a skinny, boyish build stared back. In this picture she wore a fast pitch softball uniform a size too big for her, her ears jutting out under the cap. In another picture was a hint of the person she was to become. It was a graduation picture, Betty in the red and gold gown. In the photo she stood with her parents: a heavy woman in a white suit, straight off the rack of Kmart, a pear-shaped short man with a curl in the middle of his forehead and an inexpensive Sunday suit. Betty smiled a bright beam as she looked away from the picture.

If her parents saw her at this very moment they would probably debate committing her to Broughton State Hospital. She had been working in her favorite Victoria Secret's red bra and panty set. At least she wasn't wearing her red garters that she enjoyed posing in. Betty didn't want to ruin her new clothes, even the everyday things, she'd bought upon graduation. And if they even had any idea she'd maxed out her Victoria Secret's credit card they might think that was grounds for being adjudicated. Besides being able to run around your own house nearly naked was a thrill in itself. Utter privacy and no one would ever be the wiser.

The moment made her think of her mother's toothy grin, and how she always responded, "Ooh, Lawdy! It's gonna be a good 'un."

She turned the lights off and raised the window, allowing a slight night breeze to enter.

Hands washed, teeth brushed, Betty Babbs marched down the hall, cut off the lights and fell flat across the mattress. A whiff of drying glue soaked the shadows, puffed past her pillow, and jogged her memory that 9:00 a.m. was fast approaching. In the downy dreams between sleep and awake she reached to set the alarm.

The rumbling of thunder woke her. It was Sunday morning. Betty sniffed the air, and above the budding green, the palest of emerald, veils of verdant and silver strikes waved. Her eyes sought out the scene of rugosa roses she'd plastered the night before and slowly her mind murmured pink-purple tunes much like the mourning doves' soft gurgle. A window strained open to cool thoughts that wed in a walk on the parapet and opened ears to the birdsong spills only to leave her falling down a trellis of torpor. She was unmistakably in southern pines. She smelled the wet moss and red dirt, denser air, warmer, sticky with dampness. Reminded her of an armpit. She detected the scent of males four miles away at Northwoods Baptist Church. If she hurried she could visit the church.

What better way to meet men than driving to church service four miles away? With no red lights to run she soon parked on a lot that was filling fast. Pausing to watch well dressed couples with crisp children she saw them hurry toward the red brick building. A few people clung to the rim of the empty foyer as choir music blared. But it was the greeting sign that pulled Betty in. A broadening slice of daylight reflected off the stained glass. Gray stones and beige mixed calling a welcome for newcomers. She checked her hair in the side mirror and wondered who might be inside.

Understand Betty normally didn't resort to such measures without good cause. Modern communication was the cause – computer dating. Imagine sweet southern breath paralleled by Yankee joy so radiant with a smile sparkling and bright and a voice so soft and ripe tripping live wires. When he typed on the computer screen inside she shivered against the quiver of a microphone until she received his instant message. Betty could almost hear the tinkling in Dan's verse, whirs teasing honeyed looks imagined to lyrics from a response unrehearsed. Lilts of his verbiage spurred passion, stirred whispers that drove her insane and when one exists in such animated crazes each other's words wane in fleeting fashion. The flush in high-boned cheeks was lively as he made her laugh so much. When he dumped her she hungered for the next instant message date that never came – a relationship rope burn. Call Babbs delirious.

Now aware that being dumped was poor motivation

for moving one to see Sunday's best flowers and dinner spreads. It had left her to wonder why sap oozes, and lonely souls debate serenity over a stone-carver's latest pride and why begotten passion was taken from her.

Betty crossed the parking lot, reached the front steps, thinking how she'd found herself at the pane, bristled wide-open staring up at sky's empty lot lusting wants of all her past mistakes back, how as a child she believed in Jesus, how the Old Testament delivered credo into her folded little hands that sweated beads like the purses relatives would buy and she'd fill with make-believe gifts.

Past the gravel expanse and the box hedges, a row of tall pencil pines moved in the wind, swaying in unison like a chorus of fat-bellied chorus ladies.

Beyond the top step loomed a wooden double stained glass door, nine feet high and richly detailed, halfway up she expected it to fly open, but pulled it open and there was an elderly man in a dressed down suit standing in the middle of the foyer passing out the prepared bulletin. At least his smile was genuine.

Betty looked at the bulletin, blue and ecru, read the time of each event coming next. At the top was a picture of Northwoods Baptist Church, and below some of the congregation. She thought bingo when smiles stared back. She'd done nothing, just stood there, feeling foolish, and minutes behind the older gentleman. Halfway up the walk, he called, "Here's a visitor card, and you have to fill out. Hope to see you again."

A bell chimed, reminding her she was late. Stumbling into a back pew at the final moment. So there she parked herself, staring straight ahead in the last row of the Northwoods Baptist Church, next to a woman whose Bible laid open in front of her, the pages psychedelic from highlighters.

Two hundred heads turned from staring at their bulletins, fascinated, as if Anne Sexton herself had written the Sunday news bulletin right where Betty sat.

Inside she dived into a back pew, sat on her stained seat with her feet on the floor, her knees pressed together and her hands clasped tightly in her lap. Suits stood across the room by the glass panes. In front of her blue steely hair rigidly stood and the older woman wore a green and red satin hat. The gloves and lipstick matched accordingly. Twins giggled while scribbling in the next pew, their white shirts stained by crayons. Their father shushed them as the organ played and the choir began. Their song sounded rich and reverent and several trebles lilted the morning. Although their choir robes draped over hands she still tried to check out their fingers for wedding rings. Did she mention she wasn't wearing a dress, just a nice pants suit?

The pastor's sermon was lengthy, definitely not a monotone voice. Black suited men worked the aisles, passing brass offering plates in the quiet servitude. A pewter plate reached Babbs containing tithing envelopes and her single twenty spiraled downward.

Blessed and dismissed, she shook strange hands, and then looked for her car, catching the bulletin man on the gravel. Muted conversations made their way from the back of her car. As she rounded the corner away from the church, she thought of how the older man had invited her to come back. Who was this man planted in the doorway to forever? Gently pushing the older man out of her mind, she knew there were possibly a few more churches she'd want to hit.

After services she hurried to her car, looking forward to the afternoon meeting she had with a newfound native. Tentatively they agreed to meet this particular Sunday at another mistreated lake bungalow.

A voice called out, nothing she'd consider a romantic interest, just Jerry the real-estate man.

They'd first met over the Internet, never in person, only talking to each other over the telephone about the sales process. Each had missed the other since a local attorney's office had handled the paperwork and due to each other's schedule they'd signed the paperwork at different times. It was several weeks after the discussion before they met.

She thought back to their first meeting and to her surprise he turned out to be a large well-dressed Mexicana man with a smile brighter than the polished buckles of his bright suspenders and polka dot bowtie. He was a vigorous sixty, his hair cut in a close-to-the-scalp military bristle. With his long, almost horsy face, and wide thin lips, he bore more than a passing resemblance to Charlton Heston sporting champagne colored sunglasses and a three-piece suit that could have been made of a pale orange polyester film. When she'd first met him she was startled at how his eyes looked like any other man's eyes. They were clear and direct and stared back at her with challenging self-assurance of motivational speakers and evangelical preachers everywhere.

She remembered signing the offering contract on the

hood of his Cadillac and the happiness she'd felt that within hours the offer was accepted. Later that day they'd met to sign the contract and Jerry had brought bubbly, proudly slapping a sold sticker across his blue and white for sale sign.

Today would just be a catch up meeting to make sure Betty was still exuberant about her newly purchased home and she eagerly looked forward to talking to her new friend. As expected he was waiting.

"Betty, due to lackluster sales, drooping prices, and spiking foreclosures, I'd have to say, all in all, this was a great time for you to buy – not the best time to sell, but you're now the proud owner of a lake property." Every detail seemed dappled in light, like the way Thomas Kincaid paints.

"So where do the single people hang out in this town?" she inquired. At this, Jerry frowned. It was a curious question.

"Well, Betty," he said, leaning over to brush grass clippings from his black shoes, "There's the various festivals Town Hall holds on an annual basis suckering outsiders in to spend the big bucks, plenty of community ball on Turner Street, behind the fire station, but your best bet is in the same places where I find clients." He snorted softly to himself. "I visit local area churches. It's not selling to souls that get you into trouble." Jerry explained how he'd usually rotate between Baptist and Presbyterian.

"Churches?" she asked, not sure of his meaning.

He pulled off his right shoe shaking out the grassy

contents, commenting, "You know, what you might refer to it as Bible thumping. But it always looks good to carry a Bible, just to fit in." He laughed, opened his eyes a little.

"You don't have a boyfriend? You look like the type that would have a guy."

His eyes gave her the once over, seeing an attractive shape, slim waist, and pale skin. Her mouth was soft, seemingly always inviting, and seemingly always sexy. Though she dressed casually with great simplicity there was something in her manner of walking and moving, and above all, in the way she pursed her full lips as she asked about the streets in the neighborhood that he noticed. In her blue, expressive eyes, something eager was twinkling, as she contemplated the pencil thin pines, and the symmetrical lake houses.

She flashed that beautiful partly bashful, partly goofy smile of her and replied, "Used to, he sorta dumped me."

"Well, is it sorta or is it permanent?"

She walked over to peer at a new church sign peeping from behind greenery.

"Feels permanent."

"And he did this recently?"

"By internet – instant message in one of those chat rooms. He typed he couldn't protect me anymore and added his memory was going because I had sorrows that needed drowning." He said, "His guts tells him one thing and his mind another."

Betty replied, "How do you fix something that you can't

fix?" She'd been dropped by hints, adding even the speed of light caused pain.

Jerry intrigued, listened to how she decided to start the New Year over, how she was too methodical for a crime of passion and how she explained if you run around deciding what's best for everybody, be ready for the consequences.

He thought back to his wives, and thought about how he told them he loved them for being the strong ones, and how the tables turned on him.

Secretly, he thought, maybe, it was an IQ problem. If you kill someone's love you can't help them, and how his and Betty's loves had passed between their hands – a sacred trust. Betty was definitely going to make an impact on her new community.

After this brief exchange, he leaned against his Cadillac to check out the new sign. He thanked her, and walked up the steps into the building. She sucked in her gut, held her head high and said, "Ya know, Betty, you might as well visit different churches, maybe try the Methodists next."

Monday evening while grilling chicken on her deck, and baking her infamous "Better Than Sex Cake", Betty was thinking about pewter plates, men, of men and pewter plates, and wondered if contributing to that plate would hurry God up as far as meeting the right one.

Maybe she should have dropped two twenties.

Babbs had a bad habit of talking to herself, and one poorer habit of answering her own questions. She said to herself, "Why's August so hot and lifting her with satiated sickness, the stridulated cricket's whine, the Japanese beetle's chomp-down of a drought's crop, an infested thorax of sucking West Nile mosquitoes and intense interest in television's weather degrees? Even the hummingbirds buzz red-hot wings around the absence of sweet drinking water."

Growing tired of talking to herself she lifted her ears to the world's noisy ground plans, the blood knocking boiling pots like a phyla of pygmies beating sticks.

Smoke poured from the grill, her dinner only minutes from perfection, when the cell phone rang. The room felt charged, as if a thunderstorm were near. She rose gracefully from her feet and answered the voice on the other end. The man thanked Betty for visiting Northwoods and asked if she had any questions. He introduced himself as Pastor Bob. Also added he taught the single's class if she'd want to visit morning services next time.

"You're in the singles class, then?" Betty asked.

Swatting at a green fly aimed for her dinner she told him she'd think about next Sunday. With the cell phone propped against her chin, and her shoulder molded into the screened-in-porch she listened to his explanation of how the singles met in a separate building from the main church. In the back of her mind she wondered if there was a reason for this. The fly flap dropped along with the phone on the railing after reassuring him she'd give it at least one more try. Trailing her was quiet birdsong, cars on the highway, and a coarse tractor somewhere in the backwoods.

Betty suspected there were various reasons the married and singles were in separate buildings, maybe the married discussed sex from a spiritual point of view and worried they might be overheard, or maybe they thought the single's minds were cluttered with sexual thoughts. Maybe the singles needed to repent alone, or maybe the parents worried that they were hung up on sex and would be a bad influence on say kids like the twins. Whatever the answer she was sure it had something to do with sex.

"Anyway, " Pastor Bob added, "Hope I didn't interrupt anything important. Before she thought she said, "No, just cooking out and baking my own recipe for "Better Than Sex Cake."

A pause ensued and Betty realized the blunder she'd so matter of factly shared, with the Pastor no less. Pastor Bob grinned on his end and thought of how she'd be an enchanting endeavor to undertake. On this note he once again thanked her and hardily extended the invitation for next Sunday.

2 - THE JOB

Before Western Carolina Betty had viewed her life as a prison sentence and experienced existence much as a condemned person might have. If anything the beauty of the world confounded Babbs and made her more despondent.

Finding a job hadn't been a big chore. Pulling out her wish book she fixed her index on which counties might be nice to live in and basically chose between the five points where her finger landed, hitting the internet for a copy of the local rag. Luckily, finding the newspaper job had been as easy as plucking a number from the air.

Honestly, she thought the editor, Mitch Mosley, looked past the realm of her pretty face and her hourglass shape toward possibilities and the fact that being fresh out of college would mean an entry level salary. Bluebirds could have flown out of his mouth and she would have grabbed them, knowing rare birds could be found in personal ad columns.

Even then Betty was in the process of perfecting her

past, intending to create a far better tale than one that included hillbillies and beer-bottle mosaics.

The office was practically tomblike when she stepped off the elevator, though it was mercifully cool, as if the low body count had prevented the air from rising above 62 degrees that day. Betty nodded to a few people as she walked through the cubicles that constituted offices. Mitch Mosley sat in a glass-fronted office in the middle of the room. Her workstation was behind him. His eyes wouldn't be targeted toward her. The first person to make eye contact with her at the Stanly Gazette was a heavyset man with short red hair, his round face beaming hospitality and no wedding ring. He tore his eyes off his computer screen, swiveled his head in her direction and wiped a crumb from his lips and extended a hand. He offered a smile, yellowing teeth, and big canines. She silently debated what made her uneasy, as she neared him, the fact he was short and squatty or the fact he was morbidly obese.

"No ring? Then you're in the right place."

Disarmed by the humor, she returned the greeting. "Betty Babbs," smiling briefly, then letting go of his hand.

"Your first job?"

"Yes, just moved to Stanly County last week."

He handed her a coffee cup and left Betty to greet the other employees. She was filling up with decaf when someone tapped her shoulder. And she turned to meet one blueberry-eyed Steve Cooney, complete with navy suit, vest, baby blue shirt, sculpted black hair, and a handshake five degrees too firm.

"Where and when did you arrive from?" He looked at her cautiously, almost warily, in the same way toddlers view peas. A monogrammed hankie sprouted from his vest pocket.

"Western Carolina," Betty replied.

Steve had big ears, the kind that made her think of how a dog lifts his head to sound. His line of approach was so corny she almost laughed. She understood the reason he talked down to her, like he was elevated higher and knew more – it had made himself feel better somehow. Betty's mind split the picture, two hundred pounds of flesh, a hazy aura, and a black penguin look swallowed him whole. Another image to lord over her.

Fortunately, her new gray-suited boss called them to attention. The group seized seats in the odd lot of desks. The social pattern was of women in front and middle, with males engaging the edges. If the group knew how they appeared gathered in clumps they might think they were in quarantined sections. She chose a desk behind the redheaded man she'd previously met. A latecomer hurried in, taking a seat.

"Mr. Cooney will open us," said the boss.

Babbs glanced left to the far end of the office. The glare through the pane backlit a brown haired man resting his shoulders, but that same glare prevented her from confirming the hint of a smile and a peek at his ring finger. This man had to be six feet plus, longish brown hair; coffee colored, and appeared as charming as they come. His smile spoke to her that every inch of him laid in perfection. She also knew he would be able to dazzle anyone he chose to use it on. His stance carved, and the last few minutes twisted her head. She saw how the naked light reflected up and down the length of him. He might be the type of dangerous man she was looking for. He'd caught her looking, only for a brief moment.

"First things first," Mr. Mosley introduced Betty Babbs as their newest prey. The introductions curved and were coming so fast and furious for Betty that she couldn't keep the names and faces straight. Most of the men misconstrued her last name Babbs with boobs, which she was graciously allotted. She felt the blood flood her face. She hadn't acted this lame since she was fourteen and embarrassed by her gym teacher.

Audible grunts raised behind her, well coordinated with Steve's voice, a rising tone producing a louder grunt. They all appeared perfectly coiffed and smile less, their eyes focused, for the most part, upper torso bound.

She considered turning quietly for a one-eyed peek, but to the best of her knowledge, peek eyeing wasn't allowed. After a quick and insincere nice-to-meet-ya greeting Betty's head bowed, deducing she was already behind.

Three girls grouped together behind Betty. She had the impression they were very close, and thought here were three women on a quest to find them in a world filled with false promises.

Stela Metro, the classified listing editor, was a dark-skinned girl with lively gestures, a little older than the others, and from the things Betty heard her say before the meeting, she must have been the ringleader of the group. Metro was a small woman with a dazzling, almost Cupid-like smile, and possessed eyes as blue as any Carolina sky. She appeared like a china doll of delicate porcelain, not a real woman at all. Pinched and full of light.

Seated to the left of Stela was Cookie Metstrom, her title unnamed, mainly a gopher for the news's crew, reminded her of someone from oriental descent. Perhaps she'd been an army brat. Her bones were delicate, and looked like she wasn't much over fifteen. She looked exhausted, or like she hadn't slept a wink the night before.

To the right of Stela, Goldie Beckett, another gopher for the news's crew perched. Her eyes held a mischievousness that poured out of her, something bold, a spontaneous provocation, and her posture was defiant. She was small breasted, one leg crossed set slightly back, her shoulders held high and a mocking glance that left any observer not knowing if she was serious or joking. Goldie was short, with small feet and hands, and her hair was black, tied back with a ribbon, falling barely past her collarbone. And she had dark honey in her eyes. Betty read well educated into her demeanor and noticed her voice was soft-spoken. Even though she was still young, her hairline had already started to recede.

Turned out Steve was the hotshot reporter, he covered all the major stories, carried the weight of the front page. He finished his updates, the grunting stopped, and her boss began delegating. Her first scoop was to follow the redheaded guy around the first week. He was formally introduced as Todd Wisenheimer. Unlike the tall lean ruggedly handsome Steve, Wisenheimer was short and plump. He covered the local restaurants and reported the health grades. It seemed Stanly County had more restaurants than they had churches at this point.

Closing observations followed, mentioning the upcoming Labor Day weekend. Betty had no plans for the holiday. Anxious for an introduction to the brown haired man she left her coffee on the desk and hurried toward his direction. A minute too late, his quickstep and distinctive shoulders disappeared into the parking lot.

3 - LABOR DAY WEEKEND

It was sort of like dating – just looking forward to a new day, and Betty was back at 9:45 a.m. sharp the following Sunday parked outside Northwoods Baptist. Standing in the shadows of the church foyer Gary Leatherwood watched Betty move her delicately slim shape past churchgoers already sitting in the middle pew section, his heart ached. He could tell he'd be captivated by her, if only she'd let him, and yet he was already rendered powerless.

After the church service and her dropping two twenties in the pewter plate, she made a path across the gravel in a mist of rain, using her just-found Bible for headgear.

The cell phone was ringing in the car. She's thinking maybe it's not such a good idea to do away with a landline and passing the cell number for every Joe to call. After almost turning her ankle, she shot for the phone, flipping it open.

The voice stated, "I'm from Northwoods Baptist, and my name is Gary, and would you like to share a ride next Sunday?"

Betty put him on hold so she could better position herself in the bucket seat. Two thoughts dominated her answer, the first being, "Yes that would be great. How would she know it's him?"

She gave a little laugh, and when she did, the same dimples she'd had as a girl formed on her checks. She talked to him almost all the way home. They carried on like a couple of standup comedians.

"You've already been introduced to me, you just don't realize it, I'm brown haired, broad shouldered and about a head taller than you. See you about 9:00 a.m. next Sunday, that'll give us time to talk more. Bye."

Gary thought how her voice sounded terrific, and she'd not declined his offer. She seemed to be one very coy, pretty, and clever woman.

"Zoom, zoom," she said; now she had a mission. Betty was always interested in adventure, even when she was a knob kneed girl.

Betty's second thought was she might've just found religion and planned on taking snacks to save money for the offering plate next Sunday. She could cook up her "Better Than Sex Cake" since she had the ingredients already and maybe offer the girls at the office some.

Babbs didn't give much more thought than to the fact she'd dropped two twenties into the pewter plate, and there was still two weeks left until her next paycheck. She felt like she was living in hand-me-downs, still on her knees, an alien, a beggar, a ghost lost from the old school of love. Thoughts staggered into the outer limits where alien life possibly existed while mere humans struggled. Why is it ones inner thoughts stagger back to birth? If only, Betty wasn't so scared of roadside astrology and the devil, she'd leave this naked atmosphere, satellite-ready, screaming, "Beam me up Scottie!"

At that moment Betty made a promise to begin praying regularly since it didn't seem her situation was so desperate anymore. She'd been telling God how she'd change, only, if he'd take good care of her. The promises had been many, as prayer invoked the visions of the all mighty down on his knees, hands clasped tight over hers. Tears of fear and loss still lingered, not sure her will was to commit. It's the degradation of having to imply the only sense she has is when she's down on her luck cursing a God for wanting a more normal life.

Deciding to check out more of Stanly County Babbs headed toward Albemarle. Turning into Highway 24/27 fifteen miles passed in silence. Her vehicle was riveted between five cars that spaced the passing lane to the solid lane, moving like a metallic snake from 45 m.p.h to 35 m.p.h. The mist had stopped and the breeze was fresh.

4 - WEEK TWO OF NEW JOB

Todd's car lurched into downtown Albemarle. It had been a long time since she'd rode in a stick shift Volkswagen. Watching him drive Betty realized his hair was the color of sunset. Especially, the sunsets that gloated over Uhwarrie Gap. Todd was thinking entirely in a different direction, still shocked that this beautiful girl had spoken to him, but that she'd also smiled back at him. Her blue eyes pierced the sweet country air of Stanly County. Babbs's long legs felt squeezed into the front seat of his bug. His head hurt, a prickly feeling of pressure on his eyeballs more than anything else. The impression was aggravated by southern sunshine glinting off just about everything: road signs, windshields and the chrome of oncoming cars. If it hadn't been for his aching head, the sky would have been compelling - a deep, dark Carolina blue.

He was glad she wasn't from this area, so she wouldn't have ready access to information about his tendencies toward depression and rebellion and the fact he was on "guarded duty" with the newspaper. His mind drifted to how his depression manifested in his body language and his stare was as empty as a collection plate.

Mornings he'd stand in front of a full-length mirror, stare back at himself, turn in profile and wring the fat around his middle. Love handles as some women would refer to them, not charming vanity but pure disgust veiled his thoughts. A Mormon could have preached at him for an hour or more.

"Why did you leave the mountains, land of the Cherokees, to move to our lovely little Piedmont?"

His ploy works. He's redirected Betty's attention along a scenic route that avoids thin trees without enough sap. He talks around the pen as if it's a cigarette in his mouth. The pen substitutes for a smoke.

She thinks of the pink-tinted stucco mansion on the lake, not to far from the fishing piers, and is overwhelmed by a confusion of emotions. Piers along Lake Tillery look quite different depending on the time you go there—night or day. It's always clean and beautiful. The lake is manmade and winds through Stanly and Montgomery counties. During summer months she was told by Jerry, the real estate man, tourists come to launch their boats or pontoons either to lunch or cruise the shores.

Fishermen park along the edges in hopes of catching rainbow crappies, brim, catfish or bass. It seemed there was always a fishing contest on the weekends. During the weekdays there's no trace of human presence. In the middle of the lake ovals of grass and water lilies seem to float, shafts of sunlight slant the still dark blue water.

The lime Volkswagen hiccupped around curves and over

hills, with Todd putting his foot on the gas pedal and then lifting it up, over and over.

"Did I happen to mention how, especially, nice you look today? The glows in your cheeks parade like you live in the sun." Todd inquisitively searches her eyes looking for acknowledgement, then turns toward Babbs and asks, "Do you think you came here to fall in love?"

Betty sits next to him, bursts into laughter, and extends her hand over his replying, "I certainly didn't come here to fall in love." She thinks of him as being a happy little piglet and drops her head.

He tucks the pen behind an ear, cocks his head again, and admires his smooth cuticles. His voice moves air, and is frustrated with his situation. He was conscious of a mounting anticipation, a nervous tickle in his stomach. Todd continues talking nervously explaining how he came from a family where there was always a lot of kissing. I'm a kisser from way back. She's thinking maybe a kisser of another kind.

"Seriously, Betty, I go through a case of Chapstick in a year. I've planted so many smooches and handshakes on babies, cooks, waitresses and they've all been fat-free. There's a bag of Hershey kisses in the dash, help yourself, there're nuts in the center of them."

She deposits these tidbits on the right side of her brain and the left side is thinking maybe that is why he looks like a chipmunk.

"No thanks Todd, but I appreciate it. I just don't need

to start looking like a marshmallow." She's thinking her instinct is usually correct about first impressions.

Todd couldn't help his last restaurant report was blasted because he'd horned in on the newest boxy breakfast house owned by a sassy mayor's wife. Latticework entranceways had hidden the filth thrown out the back door, much like one of the local Chinese places. A small trail of rat poop had arrested his attention and thankfully, he hadn't eaten the food. He'd avoided the details of these observations in the press, only stating these breakfast houses were popping up in the blink of any eye, blended into the history of a community like Stanly County. He figured he didn't tip the waitress, who was the owner's sister enough for his coffee. The editor was entirely engaged in selling newspapers. Most people in town paid no attention to his column anyway.

The owner had echoed claims to the editor she'd been judged on whom she was married to, and not the merit of her catering abilities. After all, his reporter wasn't the health department and seemed too high-strung and suspicious to be in the presence of the town's upper class.

Betty's thinking how the day had started out peaceful, but in rearview aspects the mirror begged broken backyard glances, each one bebop ping to heat rhythms, browning pines and squeezing sap. Three more days of one hundred degree weather and a jerking bug without air conditioning. Awareness squinted her eyes like sweet tarts.

"Todd?"

He checked his speed.

"Yes?"

"How'd you end up in such a small town? Born here, move here, what's your story?"

"Honest truth?"

"Certainly!"

He weaved back to the right lane. "More churches with single females."

Betty paused.

"To be honest, Babbs, at least twenty five single women above the age of twenty at about all of the churches."

They rolled by used-car lots, with at least a hundred red, white, and blue plastic flags flapping in the wind. They cruised along one edge of the concrete town square, past the courthouse, the town hall, and the brick edifice of the elementary school. For the next few minutes they both sat motionless, stopping for the red lights and going with the traffic. Todd dropped his shades to hide his embarrassment. Betty decided to dig her way out of this dilemma, which was most definitely heading toward his personal life and beginning to infringe on her own.

"So where's lunch today?" she asked.

Todd appeared green, almost like how his bug was lime colored and everyone referred to it as a Lime Sherbet. She made a mental note to stop by Wal-Mart and pick up a pair of solar shield glasses.

He jerked the wheel and replied, "We've arrived."

"Tiendos Mexicana Grill" glared back at her. The

outside paint blended with his car and the front addition of a blinking light stating how you could eat and pay bills at the same time jarred her frame. If that wasn't enough the flashing red/blue neon sign circled by white Christmas lights flashing "OPEN" finished the job.

"What a treat."

"Let's hope so anyway. I gotta get a good review in the paper for Wednesday." Todd gave her a sly look.

A short woman greeted them at the entrance. She was not fat but stocky, built like a defensive tackle, with a broad, dark face, girlish eyes, brown arrows shooting straight through their steps. Her flip-flops smacked against the floor. She stared at Todd and Betty for a moment, while Todd grinned an awkward grin. The woman's accent reasserted where they were.

Inside a Spanish girl dressed all in black played on a guitar and sang. The diner was small, dark, and smoky hot, the songs epic or melancholy, not many people were there yet, and before they finished their drinks Todd grasped her hand, interlacing his fingers with hers, and asked if she believed in love at first sight.

"I hope you don't mean me, you don't even know me? Maybe you mean that for a long time you've been hoping that one day a girl like me would turn up in your life?"

"But we could start by getting to know each other very well," Todd replied, very slowly, watching her reaction.

The surprise made her yank back her hand and clench it convulsively in a nervous movement. Her jerky hand flew quietly to her lap, and her stance did not show the agitation she was feeling toward him.

In the half-light, she leaned forward and her face came so close to his, he could feel her breath. Her eyes scrutinized him and glared up at him, trying to read his delirious mind.

"People in small towns mostly wed and have children and raise them. Churches here don't look at life the way city folk does. Down here, honor and self-respect are a lot more important than meeting the crunch of a deadline and sealing it with a martini lunch. Just simple people, Betty. This town looks at each other deeper than outsiders do. And they judge by what they see."

"Isn't there scripture about judging?" she retorted. "There are several about wrongs and rights as well," she informed him. "Cultures fall where the religion and arts become superfluous."

His eyebrows shot up.

"Oh, did you think I was stupid because I came from the mountains?" she asked blithely adding a sweet smile. She changed the subject before he could say anything else.

A moment later, she shot back at him, "Todd, now I know you can be a well-behaved snot-nose that can act proper. How do you think it would look for me to head straight back to the office and file a sexual harassment grievance with Mr. Mosley on my first day?" Her body shook like an iceberg about to break loose, but she remained still, passive, resigned to this effusiveness, casually turning him off with the chill. "You talk about life as if it's a calculated artifice, like a carnival game that's fixed so you always win. You are so fake and so silly that it's the closest you could ever get to any type of relationship. But you know what that's okay, and you know why? You're the one being left behind. You'll have to figure out your personal problems yourself."

Betty leaned back against the seat. "All we have to do is survive each other." She needed a night of sleep to fully recover from the emotional and physical drain that was sapping her strength.

The owner, a Mexicana/Cherokee prison-survivor had taken them on a wild ride. The sunlight flipped with his burritos, adding a taco sauce that poured strange magic down their pallets. The virgin margaritas without a doubt helped.

Todd urged her to close her eyes and dream she was in old Mexico, surrounded by taco baskets. "You won't believe what they serve for dessert -- hot pepper angel cakes. All you have to do is eat one of them and you float like an angel the rest of the afternoon."

She's thinking here's Todd and her propelled full-throttled, struggling in a real world to preserve antiquated traditions from other cultures. Maybe, the paper staff thinks she's the flighty, along for the ride type. At least she hoped her new boss didn't label his employees.

Five minutes after they left the restaurant Todd pulled into a gas station, and it wasn't to buy gas. He took quick steps toward the men's restroom marked out of order. Babbs saw him detour to the women's side. After dodging the obvious, he strolled toward the car and asked if Betty needed anything.

"No, but thanks for asking."

He muttered in gutter Spanish all the way back to the office. Betty tried to pretend she didn't comprehend one single nasty word. Todd was thinking if she did at least she didn't let on.

They rolled out of the parking lot onto Highway 52 heading west toward Albemarle.

The sun hovered just south of noon, sending yellow lasers off the windshield. Todd tuned into a local radio station, and the lyrics burped out unfamiliar tunes. He had begged for her obvious glare, but didn't have the gall to ask for her forgiveness.

After an awkward pause Babbs inquired, "So, how's this review going to read?" Glances passed between them and Betty knew it meant something, but not what.

His reply led her to revolving doors in a police-prison state. Obviously, his rain had stopped for the sake of the sun to shine. It was clear she'd lost to his claims of how fabulous the meal was. The owner's parents were drunks he told her, beating their entire family early in the morning hours. Todd explained to her the details, and of how the owner had explained the situation, and how he'd felt driven to bring culture to Norwood's mill town, because the color of his skin couldn't be peeled away.

The Mexican's escape route was much like her wish list. Dealing with all of these delusions brought Betty to the conclusion maybe she needed medication. This mixed up man said he could eat there everyday of the week, and I'm thinking this must be the way lovers live when they take on rainbows of think tanks. This ride made her think it sure beats the devil out of staying at the office. And to think, this was only Monday.

5 – SUNDAY'S CHURCH DATE

Today was the big day. Her head raced as if she'd just run a marathon. Thirty minutes had passed since the climb out of bed, and another thirty spent inhaling the lake air and coffee. White dishes on the table become blue after glancing at the time. Betty kept thinking of what's-his-name, Gary Leatherwood. She decided to dig into her closet, leave her personal life on hold for a while, and find something conservative, but appealing to wear. After pulling her wardrobe together and removing the hot curlers she combed out her hair and headed for the car. Below the steering wheel her legs twitched. She spoke to herself in the mirror, backing up between all the reverence the morning had offered and the pause of a possible date later on. And she supposed for a second she'd had the first deep conversation with her conscience. Sighing her eyes fixed on the speedometer, weaved right, cut her speed and pulled into the church parking lot.

On first glance she didn't see anyone waiting. The air smelled of crisp grass clippings and warm welcomes. It was like going out to eat, hearing the special, and deciding if you wanted it without looking at the menu. Some impulses require no considerations.

She lingered on the sidewalk until someone entered her peripheral view, someone she recognized. She supposed he might be Gary, but he was the mystery man from the office she'd tried to trail, and he appeared as if he were undressing her with his eyes. It was strange but she felt as if he were watching her. She could imagine him sitting like a panther, waiting, considering how he might block every exit before she reached it. She turned and got an eyeful of black. He clasped her hand, his over hers, and led her to the front door. The moment paused, and awkwardly, they dodged the stares as they sat middle-rowed on the right side of the church. They both thought this was going to be interesting.

Betty gave her skirt a yank, stated, "This is unbelievable and a bit amusing."

His brown eyes smiled and nodded. The choir stood, and piano music sprayed an attentive audience. The singers were countless, colorful, and staggered in height. Their voices enveloped the crowd and the minister hailed all to attention, and voices rolled forward, singing until the flow of music halted. There was a short sermon, plates passed, and the call to worship began. Morning flew, set hope atop stilts.

Gary turned at the end of service, said "Feels like dinner time. Ready to eat?" Not knowing what to expect Betty nodded in compliance. She hoped he didn't want Mexican.

They left in both cars and Betty drove straight to her house, parked, and climbed into Gary's.

"Where would you like to dine?" and Betty replied, "Surprise me." She'd even surprised herself, feeling the combination of tenderness and desire that he inspired in her.

He made a right beside the road entering her development, and paralleled the lake along a two-lane road, both lanes clover-covered and sedate, nearly vacant at midday. Toward the lakeside, the water sprouted water lilies; and turtle shells floated like endless rows of stone.

Gary slowed for the stop sign, watched two men fishing, and turned toward Main Street in Norwood. He parked his car alongside the main drag, hopped over to Betty's door, and opened it wide, saying, "and thank you Lord for getting us here."

Standing in the parking lot of black pavement, she saw a country clapboard type café, people hanging off the porch, through the front foyer, and past a couple of brown stained rocking chairs. The old rockers, creaking floorboard, tongue-and-groove walls, and the ancient habitat appealed to her. Ceiling fans on the porch outside and she'd thought only her father thought of that. She recalled how he spent hot nights on the porch watching the bug zapper electrocute the pests.

"Looks like business is good, expect a little wait?"

"Not too long." he replied.

Once inside the restaurant, stairs led to the left and to the right, a wooden banister separating customers eating from ones waiting. She felt her knees weaken, listened to the tempo of the crowd, and smelled the country cooking that tickled her sniffer. What arrested her attention was the canoe hanging from the ceiling with fish net mesh holding a mermaid that reminded her a lot of a mannequin. Her gold paint job had to be from a spray can.

Gary smiled, said, "This is our local fish camp on Friday night, our town is a little countrified."

The morning looked blue and beautiful. Looking ahead, Babbs watched a line of black suits glide past the breakfasters, flap open their billfolds and argue about who'd pay the tab. Small town life -- she was in love. Their mates squawked a little ahead of the check out line, dropped their line of sight at Betty and Gary. She felt like a flamingo on display.

Gary watched Betty as her eyes searched the cake counter one waitress was stocking for lunch. If only he could have read her mind he would have heard her thoughts about a fairy godmother waving a magic wand arranging the pumpkin pies like gorgeous coaches. There were enough pies to sell at a church bazaar. "You know Gary, it might be breakfast, but I might just have to sample some of that pie." He envisioned her as Cinderella at a ball.

"Countrified," just like he said.

Three flapjacks, two eggs over easy, bacon and toast later, the treetops whizzed by, and a low winding whistle filled the air. Blown from its habitat Betty's combed hair wrapped her chin. It held the slightest gold tinge of the sunlight and flipped back and forth with Gary's driving. Impossible to talk given the fullness, she felt her voice lift as if aboard a roller coaster. An embroidered flower flapped on her collar, its colorful lapel wavering.

The couple said only brief salutations at church and lunch. She really felt like the new girl on the block, but at least they seemed comfortable. She wondered how many other churchgoers spent their Sunday riding the lake roads.

Gary pulled into her driveway, and then turned in his seat. "So, Miss Betty, how'd you enjoy your morning?"

"Just fine," said Betty unhitching her seat belt. "And you, Mr. Gary?" Teasingly she added, "I know you'll cry, you'll miss me, and you'll think about me the rest of the day and throughout the night," gesturing her eyes in an upward fashion and a laughing lilt to her voice. "All right, there's no other way to say it, we'll see each other in the office tomorrow morning."

He reached out and caught her wrist. She was surprisingly calm and thought about how shades lifted and fell. Her scenery brightened and dimmed. Betty yawned looking forward to seeing more of Gary.

His smile answered her question, and he pulled his sunglasses back into place, and handed her his telephone number. In the next few moments, Gary, who she knew she almost liked, agreed to him calling her later.

"Tall, organized, and sure-footed," muttered Betty as they split up. "I might as well have fainted in his presence." Armed with her bible she headed for the porch, tried to remember if it was one twenty or two that had drifted into the plate that morning. She thought it was priceless to be with him, to see how his brown eyes danced when she moved, the mischievousness in his voice.

Her smile arrived like a sequined locomotive, ready to compete the sun for the brilliance of Monday's display. She thought, an odd introduction, for sure, but a decent start to her new life.

Betty paused on the porch to gaze across the lake. The sun had started to go down and red flames streaked the water. So much beauty. At times it took her breath away and she would remember this moment forever and told herself, "I really want to get to know Gary better." The memory of this Sunday hovered behind her words. Entering her new home, she thought maybe God was granting her opportunity, plus the fact that she'd been to church, on time, and for two consecutive Sundays.

Gary was the kind of man she imagined stretched out, simple as they come. Man – a.k.a. dark, dreamy and a hottie. In this moment she added him to the mix of her new life, imagining his ropy arms squeezing the love out of her, her ears pressed against his heart, soothed by the beating sound. She could stroke his dark hair, twist it gently off his forehead, make him laugh, then retrace her digits with a walk back down his broad shoulders. This was perfect, meant to be, and such a big change from the other singles she'd met thus far. "I'm caught," she uttered and hugged the chenille a little tighter around her own chest.

Her just reward was smooth still air, the edges of new beginnings merging with the afternoon. She felt that a pot of gold might suddenly appear in her path, or an elf might unexpectedly arise from her backyard. Her eyes followed the water, the evening had become leaden, with gray sky and the treat of a shower, but now, Babbs was ready to cross the playing field and feel her few stars shine. Betty grinned, impressed by Gary's bravado. It was a trait she greatly admired in others.

In this month of surprise, as the trees started to shed their leaves, and the oaks spit yellow all at once, the black squirrels in the tall wheat beyond the river searched out her eyes. Even the hornets were drilling holes in the ground, nesting in homes outside her gutter. The pines were laced with undergrowth of muscadine, something that made her think of home. The ducks on the edges of her home seemed to be paddling backwards. She couldn't be sure but emotions she'd forgotten seemed to burn right out of her, and she'd forgotten how much she'd missed them. Surely, Stanly County was the place that would offer her happiness, a steady job, and a future husband. Why was it she felt so reluctant, as though she'd backed into this town?

6 - A NEW WEEK

The morning meeting was hardly over when the boss did a war dance, signaled Todd and Betty to his office. Mitch Mosley was a bulldog and this paper was his life. Guilt moved them, although, she wasn't quite sure what they were guilty of doing. Littering observers looked mute, empty, and knots of red silence circled the oncoming hour. She unfolded her legs, and stepped forward. There was a mischievous grin in his eyes. She wondered if she could ever be Miss Sunshine.

With his pointing finger, Mr. Mosley pushed his feet, one at a time, to the center of the room. He told us he'd tell us where to go from this point.

"There's nothing do you, hear me Todd, nothing you do that I can't hire someone else to do!"

Babbs would have cried a river if he'd spat those words toward her.

Todd, who didn't appreciate the superior tone of his boss any more than he was inspired to take orders. He came out of his tortoise shell, questioned with a voice that would level Egyptian pyramids, "What did we do wrong?" At that moment Betty knew Todd was impossible to embarrass. He didn't know the meaning of shy.

Their boss pushed up his head, talked nonstop, covered a dozen different episodes (which she had no part in) for what seemed an eternity. Sounded like he'd been along for the ride and henpecked each restaurant Todd had visited. Betty didn't want to draw attention to herself, and figured it was the Chinese's working minds. They didn't like how Todd had explained his view of trash departing the back doors.

Mitch leaned back in his chair and all the humor went out of his face. Betty looked as solemn as Mr. Mosley. This was serious business. She drew in a long breath. Babbs was thinking every job had at least one mental case and she'd been saddled to him.

When he finished talking, he sat back and locked his hands over his head, satisfied with the show he'd given. He mapped out our week, giving us time to take it all in. Then he looked Babbs in the eyes, grinned and raised his eyebrows. He had high arched, Dr. Spock eyebrows, which he used to great effect, like he had posed.

"Well, what do you think?" But his eyes told her that she knew that anything he said would be great.

Todd, not paying much attention weaved, stitched his probation around a shaky ground. Betty thought of how he'd been confined, his eyes darted back and forth, landed on a flower, the way honeybees meld hives. The scene was a view of what was expected. Todd lived dangerously. Now it was easier to understand why Mitch Mosley had decided to give him assignments. The more Betty thought about it the more agitated she'd become with Wisenheimer.

He waited, stretched his arms across his chest, arms loaded, and grinned ear to ear, that solid row of yellow teeth. Reminded her of a cornfield. Like he'd just hit the jackpot in Las Vegas, then he scuttle-butted upward, his middle pressed hard against the conference table. And then she realized for sure he was a con. Despite the way he'd caught her off guard before, Betty still had the ability to foresee, and saw this job wasn't exactly his forte. Her eyes were opened like the Fourth of July fireworks.

Todd laughed, "He's a bit sensitive towards me. I think Mosley thinks I'm Satan. But then he's never met Satan." Chuckling, he talked on and on, before finally leaving. Today was going to be a buffet feast.

He rattled charm Babbs's way, and his insistent talk kept her from being rude. Thank goodness it wasn't her that Mr. Mosley was disappointed with.

"God awful," spilled out Todd's mouth. "Hateful people, those Chinese. He explained how he'd given them free advertising and what did they do, complain."

We plopped ourselves in the bug and followed Highway 52. Todd pulled out a flattened cigarette pack he kept in the dash. Then he held the pack out to her.

"Want one?" he said.

There was one cigarette left in the pack. "Don't smoke," she said.

"Worried it will kill you?" he laughed, as he lit up.

"Yes," she said and watched the smoke curl, flicking the flame. The heat outside was a few degrees hotter than their meeting inside. He held the filtered stick between his thumb and pointing index finger, leaned forward like he was meeting the cigarette partway each time he puffed.

She looked out the windshield and straight into the sun, a golden hole punched through the sky, a bright and pitiless spotlight pointed into her face.

"Oh yeah," he said as if just remembering where they were to go. He pulled out a county map, where he'd no doubt tell her where to put it. Betty studied the map, followed the roads from Highway 52 to Old Ellerbe Road, the location they were heading for -- Ellerbe Springs Restaurant. This establishment heralded the esteem of time, and was founded in 1948. It's a sprawling southern mansion, converted to a bed and breakfast, offering a buffet lunch to the public. Todd coughed, held his hand to cover the smirk of our next assignment. Either he was dumb or just plain rude. Maybe he didn't care. Point is, a blank space there, or anywhere means one of two things: Either he'd never visited the place or, if he had he was ashamed of his last behavior.

Rolled green circled the square-trimmed boxwoods surrounding this enormous establishment, double door entrance, and elongated windows. Below were elegant window boxes with perfect plants. Something had a hold on Todd's brain, what Babbs didn't know. Time passed quietly with their meal. Everything ran meticulously like a well-oiled engine. In, serve, out, pay. They couldn't have expected anything better.

Todd examined the ticket, and Betty said, "The waitress

certainly deserves a twenty percent gratuity." He nodded, and they both smiled; his footsteps echoed hers. She plopped herself on the bug and waited.

Without intending too she'd driven into a landmine. He was peeved about their orders. Todd never told her how much the tab was, the amount of the tip or how he planned his review. He chitchatted in totally another direction, and Betty didn't see the humor of what he was sharing.

"Gabriela Martinez, can you imagine?"

Betty asked, "What are you talking about?"

He chuckled and laid out the local gossip of her and Gerald Martin, the one who inherited the business and she the money. Two Martins and he shared his thoughts of how he'd never met a Martin of any culture he'd liked.

"You ever hear tales of her?"

"No, I'm not from this area."

"Well they are married now, and the noise has subsided. So the story goes she'd laid everything in Ellerbe except the linoleum."

"That's more than I need to know," Babbs whispered. She didn't want to satisfy Todd's need for petty gossip.

Betty looked at his face, witnessed firsthand his telltale soul, and emphatically, reminded herself if it wasn't time to ask the boss if the new hire shouldn't be getting acquainted with the remainder of the team. Who cares how wild a romance can land someone a spread like they had? Both are happy and successful.

"Take a good look," she said to Todd. "He did the first time he went around the block," he replied.

Betty retorted, "Are you planning on driving us in circles all day?"

Here they were in the middle of a brickyard, and the sun is going down. She'd just bet there were a lot of firearms discharged in the nightlife of town limits.

He'd gotten her completely off track, and she spied his routine clearly. Betty felt no additional time in route with him would be necessary. But she knew when to open and close her trap. They talked about the paper, and the quiet between them became unspoken words. The car seemingly on autopilot sailed into the working lot. She had fallen a few steps behind him, was regarding him with a look of unhappy disgust before both of them wished the other good night and see you later -- tomorrow. Babbs looked back once more to see him watching her. Todd was such an authority on everybody she hoped he wouldn't start any gossip about her life. She hated the smile that crossed his face just as he was about to spill his guts.

Her existence did a somersault that day. She noted different observations, wore a jacket and skirt each workday she was assigned with him, one that covered her curvy shape, and lived in her small cubicle after returning to the office in the afternoons.

At home things were serene, and for the moment she was overwhelmed. This week she'd been rocketed cross-country in a bug, eager to elbow other tourists to eye-in the bottomless gorge of her heart. The view evoked oohs and ahs, obligatory to a sense of beauty.

Everything was too big, too small, the day tinted wrong, or maybe, she's just in the wrong place. Betty stared in consternation at the venetians, which seemed to flick open and shut. A mosaic picture bleached in tea colors. Babbs put her thoughts to bed, so a laminated day of new sights would soon be dangled in front of her.

If she could lick the problem of moving out of the mountains she could navigate through the issues with Todd Wisenheimer. Betty glanced toward the kitchen. Baking always soothed her frets. Noticing the time she decided to make her infamous cake. What was so hilarious was the name her college roommates had dubbed her recipe. "Better Than Sex Cake." Every time she baked one the honor dorm men located on the floor below their dorm drifted upward. Any other time they had their noses in a book. She smiled about the ways the girls had her snorting in laughter. But it's a great cake and the name was one for sure conversation. As she pulled the flour, eggs, vanilla, pineapple, whipped cream, coconut, and other ingredients together the thoughts of work drifted out the window and paddled upstream. She'd never share her recipe with anyone but she would let them know the name of the scrumptious-delumptious cake. On that note she took out a decorated nameplate type card and wrote "Better Than Sex Cake" in calligraphy.

7 — DYNAMITE IN PLAYING FIELD

Tuesday was beautiful, but absent from the sun. The office was buzzing when she arrived, her cake in hand. Unnoticed she decided to leave it next to the coffee pot, removed the foil and placed wax paper across the square. On top of the wax paper she placed the decorated name card. Betty smiled humbly, thinking they should at least know what they are eating. No one would be able to clearly see through the paper, but would be able to know what a treat it was. Around 10:00 a.m. she'd offer everyone at break a piece of cake. It was going to be a good day. Shortly after booting her computer up and starting on the emails she looked up and watched the glass window in front of the break room. The girls had lined up, peering shyly in to the break room, acknowledging the action taking place. The room was full of men encircling Todd. Todd stood with a piece of "Better Than Sex Cake" in each hand and several of the guys were trying to get him to give up one of the pieces. It was pandemonium. The office staff was wild. Mitch Mosley broke the party up by seizing one of the slices from Todd, and only after inhaling the piece ordered everyone back to work. Betty covered her smirk.

The magic of cake. She was glad she brought a disposable cake pan because she'd never own up to bringing it after that mob scene. And to think it wasn't ever break time yet. But not before she overheard Todd's incomplete phrase about Babbs being "peculiar" about men. God knew what that meant.

Her boss, Mitch Mosley, decided it's time to move ahead. The remainder of her week would be spent with Bernard Bakes, Sports columnist. Mr. Mosley went into great depth to explain what an extensive four-week search had been held to find Mr. Bakes. The paper had focused on three prominent candidates and finally hired Bernard. Bakes had left his home state and alma mater of Tennessee to accept the North Carolina job. He brought the no-huddle spread offense to the paper that he'd helped to invent at Tennessee when he coached. Her boss explained the success the paper had with increased circulation because of the sport pages.

Bernard Bakes was on vacation when she arrived. The nice thing was he didn't live far from her. They, actually, lived less than a mile apart. Mr. Mosley had informed her he made surfing on Lake Tillery look like child's play: Macho is a universe of single girls for him. Betty didn't know his denomination of faith yet, but definitely intended to find out. She'd figured him for a local.

In bright green slacks he joined her. He explained how they would sail through this week. His tan was dark and his stride confident. Waves on the lake, from what she'd been told, were normally little more than ripples.

But as a behind schedule morning crashed through afternoon high-speed thunderstorms loomed. They'd been assigned to get the scoop on what Coach Smiley had to say about the last two recruits being arrested on misdemeanor charges, and if they'd be allowed to play Friday night against another local 2A team. When the three of them met, she'd felt like she'd peeled off her clothes, waded water to waist deep, and lunged into warmer streams than expected. Drops of his verbiage rocked her soul, so she lunged again.

Bakes sat on the maroon–and–gold turf, his golden blonde hair flopping down across surfer eyes. Waves of his hands swelled and began to roll. With quick bursts he popped to his feet, tilted left, then right, shoving resistance toward the coach and gained full-throttle speed toward the tip of the day. Coach Smiley stood cool.

"They can do this, Bernard," said Smiley, bobbing his ears. "The team can't drown and have their flesh eaten by the cannibal team".

Those boys are young, maybe stupid, but this community needs to give them a second chance like he planned on doing.

Little did they realize the school had proffered up their legal aid and talked turkey with the district attorney earlier that morning. Another paper already had that scoop.

"What's next?" Bakes inquired.

"We play ball, not call foul."

Coach Smiley was certainly suited for his name. For a moment, she'd felt the catch of a big kahuna. His arms were deeply tanned, his hands dry and weathered. Betty sprawled his meaning, and reality rushed in defense: the gurgle in her stomach filled with politics, the bitter taste simmered her tongue, and the newness of seeing small town turfs surfaced at many levels. In steady rhythms, the boys humped the field, started push-ups toward the opponents. Bernard said, "We needed to hear both sides." Babbs felt like a foot pivoted her backside down, but felt the slow release allowing her to rise back to her knees, wobbled once, and heard the roar of the upcoming crowd.

Her hand tugged at her pantsuit, lifted her left foot into his black SUV, her back landed toward the rear, and her throat rejected local politics. Neon swirled above Betty's head and she shot to the surface.

"How's that for you?" B.B. asked.

"Simply unbelievable," Babbs wrangled back. He raced the engine roughly, in the same manner as a hippo being submerged in water. Bakes pushed the pedal hard, floated a couple of miles above the speed limit to the next school.

"Betty, don't worry about the speed," he said after noticing her eyeballs curving his way. "I've maintained this self-imposed 9 m.p.h. over the speed-limit for a while, not getting a ticket, jacked up the air pressure in my tires, and promise to get you there safe and save gas mileage."

"Don't look directly into W.T.'s eyes when we interview him. You'll feel like you've encountered a shark."

"Never ask him questions, let him do the talk and the walk." Bernard Bakes's smile dripped honey.

Betty looked at the gray-blocked field, now filled with various players, equipment, and plenty of Gatorade.

"Unbelievable," he said.

In a forge of backlighting he shook off sweat that looks to her like sparks. W.T. and Bakes turned petty in the heat. The debate was like vultures hanging over the good kids. It was nothing, just an argument. She hung her arm out for the ultimate burn to someone untouchable. Regardless burnt skin sings when it finally hits cool.

They decided after meeting with him, they both needed a clean shower, and were off the field in fifteen minutes. Bakes stated, "Not a world record with him."

On the way back he mentioned the close distance they shared between homes. She still wondered about his level of faith, girlfriends, and other trivial details. Jutting out the lakeside, a fishy escape caught them off guard. They spotted the restaurant sign and pulled off the road. Though it was nearing two o'clock in the afternoon the parking lot was crowded. Betty tried not to grimace. Bernard stated how he loved this fish place. After parking a half-mile away, slipping past the lifesaver mounted porch we brushed our feet on rope-like rugs. The restrooms were clean and they were seated immediately. A very young man with a long ponytail, and as straight as a horse's tail, was delighted to serve us. Seafood scents filled the air, and it was lunchtime. Betty squinted to see the far end of the parking lot, the porch buzzing with conversations.

Young people moved along the scrimmage, refilling hushpuppy baskets and pouring tea. They recited specials as if timed by a stopwatch. Strangers nodded heads their way, and chimed in hello. Bakes replied, "And hello to you too stranger. Meet my newest companion." She wondered if they thought another girl or work buddy.

The buffet stretched across the middle of the restaurant. She's assessing how many calories she's going to have to burn off tonight. The line fused forward, Betty grabbed an oval plate, and then heard singing ahead at a table for ten. Bad singing, but it was singing none-the-less. She recognized it — the same cheer sung during sporting events when the home team is ahead by numerous points. A bald man in a purple and maroon sport's shirt led the ensemble. "Nah-nah, hey-hey, we're on our way." The chorus repeated and she stepped forward to observe a better view. Even the head cook, a large country type, heralding a fisher's hat stood with a fork in each hand, holding up the catch of the day, which was lobster. He reminded me of a symphony conductor with a spear gun. She blushed slightly at the entire group – all men and each more redheaded than the next proceeded to raise beer mugs and smile. They didn't look like cooks; they looked like a rowing team. An inebriated group at that.

The voices in the buffet line joined in, and she had to admit there's a Piedmont charm in singing eulogies to seafood. The cook grinned, performed a perfect about-face, and the fork doomed the lobster to boiling heights. She reached for more tails when the edge of someone's plate poked her rib.

"Betty Babbs! Imagine this, we're all dining together." It was Todd. "Surprise, surprise."

Bernard sarcastically said, "Skipper, you've always had an incredible gift for showing up in the wrong place at the wrong time."

"All I'm doing is my job, Bakes. It's not my fault."

She couldn't think of anything to say. Her plate was full and he lingered above the tails, began picking up ones she'd left, stacking them slowly into a pyramid until the words rolled up, "Let's all sit together."

Todd slurped his tea that had a lemon peel curved delicately in its folds of ice and slurped raw oysters from their shells and scooped up oyster crackers by the handful. Betty stared.

In the mountains seafood was rubbery, and fish restaurants were few. Betty borrowed the claw-crusher from Bakes, crushed the shell, and out of nowhere it turned somersaults landing in Todd's dish. Talk about embarrassed; Babbs didn't think the moment would ever end. He'll probably write about the episode and she'd be gossiped about for next week's news.

Todd elbowed Bernard, and we all bowed our heads, and whispered simultaneous amen's. A good sign, maybe Bakes did attend church.

"So you married?" Bernard questioned. "Ever been married?"

She turned, added more sugar to the tea, and nodded a no. "You married, ever been?"

"Yeah, once. Never again." He'd felt he gotten married and divorced so fast it was like something out of The Time Machine.

In silence both reached for the tartar sauce. Although, Betty believed they were both thinking about the other? Of course, by now, she's thinking the entire religious sect in this area is crazy.

Todd agreed with Bakes's sentiment. Betty was totally shocked after having heard of his reasons for living in Stanly County.

A young male waiter appeared, asked, "Dessert?" Then questioned if they needed refills on our drinks, managing to smile a little more brightly at Babbs than Bakes or Todd.

They all shook their heads no. "Separate checks, we've each our own expense account."

Bernard turned and caught her staring. His eyes danced in her direction for a second as he smiled, and laid the tip down. Todd rolled his eyes, folded his arms over his chest in mock annoyance for an overabundant gratuity. Betty's learning Wisenheimer is a cheap skate. This brief stunt left her feeling more and more like he was someone desperately seeking attention. Bakes stated they'd check out the high school fields on the drive back to work. He left her passing the ball just west of sunset.

Tooling down Highway 52 in the right lane at a fuel-efficient 54 m.p.h. in a 45 m.p.h. zone we came up on another black SUV. Another black SUV? Of course there are other vehicles like Bernard's vehicle, but Betty had already glimpsed the driver. It was W.T. Smiley.

Bakes said, "Seriously some guy is doing my gig, 54 m.p.h. and we need to get on back to the office. "He's stolen my thing!"

Betty held on tight as Bernard passed him to the right in the exit-only lane (without accelerating, of course, because that wastes gas) and looked him over real good. Coach Smiley slid by at the breakneck speed of 54 m.p.h. sizing up the competition. Bakes was determined to reclaim his mantle as king of the 9 m.p.h. road king rule this afternoon. He looked at Betty and said, "Can you imagine that Smiley?" "There's no sense burning gas to get to a stop sign faster, right?"

Betty's eyes zoomed around Bakes and Smiley and wondered if she was going to get back to the office in one piece. Apparently, there was as much competition off the field as there was on.

"You hate drivers like me, don't you Babbs?"

Trying to make a joke out of a building situation she replied, "Maybe one day, someone will figure out a way to supplement gasoline with the processed grease left over from cooking oil. Then you want have to creep up to your 9 m.p.h. over rule."

Bakes is thinking she even talks restaurant crap. Mosley didn't go wrong hiring her, thinking about how Todd had been laying out several days a month now. Seeing how distracted she's become he changes the subject.

"Penelope," Bakes said. Betty watched his face sober, something inside him sigh, "She got killed. The girl you replaced." His lips were a shade of blue, and he appeared to be hardly breathing.

"How long ago?" Babbs inquired.

"Six months."

His eyes flicked and his brows arched, shot arrows past the windshield and he decided to talk in another direction.

Sudden bursts of sadness erupted the air and Betty couldn't pull the trigger of her thoughts back.

"What happened?"

But he pressed his hand out like a stop sign. "Crazy, wild, we both went to the same schools, were the homecoming king and queen, and she constantly ruffled the feathers of our church based community. When we were in middle school, we stole candy bars from the Food Lion, gobbled them down while walking the train tracks on the wrong side of town. She was my best friend and she ruined my life, even though she said I ruined hers."

Betty nodded, smiled, and witnessed the sad picture of loosing one's best friend. She turned her face to the window, and she heard Bakes inward sigh, making little damp choked sounds, which evened out to a regular conversation.

"You know, I even helped her land the job that was her death. Her and Cookie, don't know if you've met her yet, were on the way to check out the county fair, past Highway 52, when the First Methodist's elderly minister had a stroke, wheeled out of control, and crashed into Penny's side. At least it was instant, no agonizing pain. But you have to move on. Maybe we can become good friends?"

Betty nodded again. Bernard pulled the SUV into the parking lot and deposited her on the gravel. He'd gotten her totally off track. She felt the sadness linger with the sun, and she held her hand out to him, offered him condolences. She opened her mouth to reply and found she had nothing to say. Betty was not used to the sensation of grief.

"We'd better say goodnight, just thought you needed the skinny in case anyone mentioned the past."

Babbs let the quiet between them become words. She closed her eyes, withdrawing into herself. A dimple appeared between her small eyebrows, a little thought line.

"See ya in the a.m." he said and backed out the drive, smiling a wide witty grin.

It occurred to Betty it's all a story. She really didn't know anything more about him than when she'd first seen him. It wasn't just that she'd found out about the tragedy, but felt the darkness one feels when questioning their faith.

On the home front things appeared quiet, dimming slowly. She gathered her observations, bent over and concentrated on her work so far. It was a quarter past ten when she looked at the clock.

She should have gone to bed then, but instead sat in front of the bay window watched the moon's surface and pondered on thoughts of how she would have reacted. Though she didn't want to think it, she knew what Bernard thought of every time he looked her way. Glancing back at the 1:00 a.m. hour she shuffled to bed.

She prayed to God to give her something as beautiful as a poem that would render the soul to stand alert, just a small token that would pull her through this shadow.

8 – THE HOT SHOT REPORTER

Steve Cooley had been married, but for all his clever moves his wife had left. And the way she'd left was a sensitive subject; the subject sidestepped most of the town. He'd been in law enforcement, had pulled his wife to over, and ticketed her for not wearing a helmet. She'd rode a Harley and her red hair blinded him. So much so that he proposed to her a week later. It was a three-year affair. He'd given everything, and she'd fallen in love with another biker. His timing was wrong. She split in the beginning of the fourth year, leaving him with two small children, one a baby, tiny and still in diapers.

"A penny for your thoughts Betty Babbs?" Cooley smiled.

She thought about his hard luck, his complicated life, and pushed her own battle with hard times and poverty to the back burner.

He continued talking, "Stanly County is a point of view, unique and even strange at times." His voice lilted her to the future. "Look at the life, the energy of our community.

Have you seen it yet?" Steve's voice had a calming effect. Betty thought he's correct and wished secretly he viewed her in such positive tones. Trust was an important issue and she was determined to exert her best side. She lifted her head, eyes flashing a bright blue in the weak light of the morning.

Cooley opened his mind to her, opened his mouth, lifted his tongue and let it roll, "I'm not from a rich family, but the wealth I've found here is very gratifying." Steve was grounded in the world of the real and ordinary. She thought he's brilliant, no wonder he's the hot shot reporter. He'd favored her with a lopsided grin, lifted the serious thoughts from her flashing eyes. The smile alone had triggered something inside her, maybe a little mystery, setting off a swooping sensation in her stomach.

For an older man he had charisma. The sensation was unnatural and made Betty's heart race.

He flipped around to her, his face corner crinkling, and said, "Wonder what kind of trouble we'll get into today?"

Babbs could have hugged Mr. Mosley after being riveted from one extreme personality to another.

She sat up straighter, leaned her back onto his leather car seat and grinned. He smiled peevishly, and added, "You're in store for a treat today."

Steve dragged her to a park away from the office. She felt as if she'd crossed an invisible divide. "Why hadn't she been told about this great place already?" she asked. His wavy hair and bright eyes challenged her, and she loved his flamboyant appearance and unmistakable way of speaking.

He was a turkey, gobbling up her aspirated exclamation about the beauty that hit her like a whirlwind.

It was very early and the red disk of a moon appeared to be in flames, taking its leave with blazing beams and the sun rising in fiery light. The fever of the geese fixed her gaze on the fountain sprouting out of the middle of the pond. She felt like she was peering in the windows of a party to see how people danced, and how people walked, so free and easy. They bent their knees, moved their shoulders, the chests, breast, and bottoms to a waltz around the concrete sidewalk.

No one was allowed to be near the pond, as there was an ornate green-coated wire fence zigzagging the edges. The geese were truly confined to a paradise. The park was a gigantic garden, with multi-colored flowers, raised bush beds, and its tiered land. She pictured swarms of walkers after work, beehives of people swarming in to eat sandwiches and shoot the breeze at lunch. Through this portal a group of very beautiful women approached, coming forward to greet them with condescending smiles. Steve pointed out that Betty was the newest game in town.

After fifteen minutes of nonstop talking she encouraged him back to their work assignment. They strolled the cement twist around the manmade pond and paced with the other walkers of the morning. They both found peace with the sunrise. It seemed too soon to leave, but they were both on the job.

She felt the crowd would pleasure in her gossip and add more detail and coloring to her story. She thought, maybe it would be an awesome rumor.

Betty hoped Penelope's passing would soon be replaced with memories of her adventuresome spirit. But she knew Steve kept her in his memory, and these thoughts evoked him at different times with her impish laughter and admiring glance from the past.

On the approach en route for Albemarle, Steve explained, "The park land was donated by one of the older families in the community. He'd been a dairy farmer and his son elevated to the position of a successful

auctioneer. Next thing the community had heard about was the farmer's death and the bequeathal of this huge acreage of land to the town for a special purpose."

His eyes shrunk back to the color of blueberries and his hair, once blonder waved silver tints beneath the baking sun. "I remember the cows and the barbed fences when I was a boy, didn't live far from the mill hill."

"Strange" Babbs murmured, not placing him in that position. She swore he turned and winked at her, like he knew all of her secrets.

Cooley tuned in a local radio station, the lyrics lazy and country-woven, making Betty want to be under an old oak and quit the busyness of life. Horns blared ahead, engines revved, and from the top of Fisher's Bridge, over the fish signs, she saw a long row of tractor-trailers, cars, and assorted vehicles. Her eyes crossed the pasture. The ground was eye level but she knew if she tramped the long dry grass she'd feel the rise and fall of undergrowth, the broad furloughs a plough had once carved. The clearing looked cultivated, but not in the memory of anyone living.

They sat twenty minutes where there was no view, and the sound of the radio joined the roar of people's complaints.

"Looks like a developing story. You man the car and I'll jog up ahead." She blinked in the sudden blinding daylight and saw Todd across the pasture. About a half city block in front of him a figure appeared in a white suit, sprinting along the pasture ruts. It was Steve in his pale colored suit, or either an ice-cream man in training for the one hundred yard dash.

The only direction they could go was forward, as there wasn't room to turn or back up. Betty kept checking the rear view mirror for clues. She rolled the window down, and took a deep, supple breath of Stanly County. The winds of autumn stirred dust on her sun-baked heart. Stagnant water stood in ditches on the side of roads breeding mosquitoes. The same autumnal winds delivered the smell of fresh road kill; the reek of hot asphalt painted the houses, choked her lungs and stained everyone's soul.

It would soon be late autumn; the last glowing leaves clinging to liquid gold maples.

Inside the car, she sat on pins and needles, hoping everything was okay ahead, maybe just roadwork or a traffic jam from a broke down car. The air felt crisp, and she flipped through the radio channels, listening for brighter music.

Moments later Steve flung open the car door, faked a shiver, and then wiped the sweat off of his forehead with the bottom of his polo shirt.

"Seen anything yet?" she asked.

"Just a number of blue lights and a couple of fire trucks. The volunteer fire department members are waving back the crowd. No telling what's going on.

I'm going to buzz the office and see if they can get Tom Martin in the chopper, and capture the full picture." He held his cell phone up, moving around, trying to find a signal. Betty thought about the commercial on TV, where the man asked, "Can you hear me now?"

"Never mind – Tom's in the air, there's the news chopper. Maybe, he'll get the scoop and we can get the story in for the paper tomorrow."

His excitement was contagious and Babbs felt the thrill she'd been searching out. Traffic slowly thinned as they edged toward Albemarle. As they eased along Highway 52, they saw the ambulance coming towards them. Steve slowed, let it reach the curve first, and followed the vehicle over the hill. Fish billboards faded from view, the terrain changing from bright to dull. The blue Carolina sky filled with a smoky haze.

"Holy crap! Is that Todd Wiseasses' car?"

Betty turned, searched the riverside community of Norwood where brick homes set high atop stilted scenery.

At the next curve she saw both lanes, vacant in the middle. To the right of the road there was a lime bug sprouted in wheat or either a soybean field, upside down. She saw a heavy man, topsy-turvy hanging by his seatbelt. The red head shined. It was hard to make him out clearly in the distance, beneath the yellow shine of sky, where clouds glowed like banked embers. His ears looked almost level with his shoulders. The long pink strip of his tongue hung obscenely from his mouth. The sight of him was a galloping shock, a jolt to her nerve endings.

They slowed, watched three volunteers reach the ambulance as the rear doors opened with a steely chatter, and drag a stretcher and a huge saw to the scene. They were sawing with a buried frenzy. "Two hours, fifteen minutes" one of the men yelled, and added, "Did you check his blood pressure again?"

Sitting no more that a couple of city blocks from the accident, Betty viewed the house with a guttered crow's nest, someone on the front stairs, another person in the screened porch area, and a couple of others in whitewashed rocking chairs. Before she realized Steve Cooley was at the side of the commotion, had his tape recorder out, asking questions at jet speed. She felt a chill crawling on the flesh of her arms. Outside the screened porch she saw the men. They were snickering.

Her eagle eyes diverted to the gathering Chinese talking at the far corner of their home. The Chinese stood their ground, peered at Todd with a calm but intense expression of a research doctor discovering a new strain of Ebola. They reminded her of seagulls squawking, as her line of sight moved from their outlines to Steve's figure. The porch of the house was narrow and crooked, the screens visibly warped, rusty and bellied outward. Past the porch was a muddy hog pen, two huge-sized pigs in it. The pigs were even peering at Todd, their squashed-in snouts benevolent and snorting. Babbs thought lime green and pickles had a lot in common.

Two medics knelt beside Todd, gloved their hands

and gently positioned him, lifting his head back gently. "Significant head lacerations, hotdog jamming his throat," one medic stated. The other thrust his fingers into his throat to unblock the airway. His partner set up the oxygen, talking into a CB radio. She wanted to run, get back to Steve's vehicle and thought please let him be alive. She noticed Todd was heaving breath.

A female medic shouted out, "There's a helicopter coming. Where's the best place to land?"

"How's he doing?" Steve asked. The female medic shrugged, "Probably should be dead."

They listened to sirens round the curves, watch the lights turn into the field, closer and louder. Two state troopers, much too close together, braked, sent grass flying. The passenger door of the patrol car opened and Bernard Bakes stepped out. His stature tall and blonde hair combed back. He walked toward her. Betty stood still. They both stared at Todd.

A bulge in his cheek, suggested something trying to escape. Betty raised her penciled eyebrows.

Bernard boarded the copter with Todd and the medical staff. The chopper rose, turned for Charlotte flashing lights.

Soon Steve and Betty whizzed toward the office, and a hot wind whistled through the windows. Blown from its habitat, a scarf wrapped her chin. Impossible to talk over the speed, even though they were both in the front seat, Steve was on a mission and Betty was just along for the ride. An embroidered parrot flapped on her shirtsleeve, it colorful beak all aflutter.

Running into the news's room they were greeted with brief questions and Steve jumped into action. Betty really felt like the new person, but at least she was in tow. She wondered if all the people lived in fast pace where she'd landed.

Entering Mr. Mosley's office, Steve yanked a stubborn recorder from his satchel, turned it on and their boss pulled his glasses up, as if that would help his hearing. Betty reached into her purse, pulled out her notes, and handed each of them a copy. She'd ample time to duplicate while waiting on the road.

Cookie, Goldie and Stela smashed the door, jolted the others to a stop. They stuck their heads into the space between the doors to listen to the talk. Betty's arms were tingling. Round oh's vegetated around the office's doorframe. "Poor guy, he's a goner," and without hesitation the entire scene erupted into what reminded her of a food fight, an odd introduction to the three girls for sure.

Mitch Mosley darted into action, sending each of them off to do a specific chore.

Betty heard Mosley's voice climb and ask the air why the idiot was even on that stretch of road. He'd sent him in an opposite direction.

Stela Metro met Betty at the elevator, evidently in a rush to get her assignment done. Her pierced tongue greeted the newcomer with large eyes.

Stela was in her thirties, pretty, hair streaked blonde,

parentheses around her mouth. She wanted to stay behind, but Stela was doing flip-flops trying to get the gossip on the accident. Her tongue curled out cold words, "Todd is in so much trouble."

"No kidding," said Cooley, setting down his satchel. "With Todd, the danger is part of the attraction."

"Doesn't anybody care if the dope's hurt?" Babbs softly spoke. Both looked at her and rushed forward into the elevator.

"You coming?" Steve asked.

With no answer to his question Betty stepped in with a wrong foot forward. In all of her mind's recall she'd never come to the unspoken suspended so close to her rear.

"We care, but Todd is on thin ice as it is," stated Steve Cooley. Steve looked troubled. "Losing a job can make a desperate person more desperate," is all he offered. "We've all told him to keep a lower profile. He seemed uneasy."

In the moment he hesitated Stela nodded and Betty thought more about her wagging tongue. The piercing darted in and out.

Steve asked Babbs, "Could you take the company errand truck or your vehicle and go check on him at the hospital?" She agreed, ready to scoot out of this atmosphere that was beyond her disbelief. With gas prices so high, she grabbed the keys to the company vehicle, hooked them over her little finger, and wiggled before turning and walking around the corner of the building.

Goldie asked Steve, "Do you know if Todd is seeing

anyone?" He shrugged his shoulders, and Betty said she don't think so, and then preceded to tell them that Todd was involved in community churches full time, and not for the reason they would love to hear.

Babbs mashed the pedal, and the monster truck lunged onto Highway 52. She continued through town, smaller vehicles gave way in the passing lane, and she felt like she was on a first date, heading into a bigger city than she'd ever been in. At Charlotte Memorial Hospital she pulled to the curb. Sunlight glinted off the hood.

Betty fiddled with the keys, and then stepped down, almost twisting her ankle. She thought, "Well, at least I'm at the hospital." She jaunted over the curb along a tangle of bushes at the edge of the parking lot.

The receptionist smiled at Babbs, shot her a wry glance. "I'm looking for Todd Wisenheimer," she explained. After identification and pressing a buzzer the receptionist pointed her in the direction of the trauma emergency room. Once inside Betty saw it was a very busy day. Paramedics were wheeling gurneys, doctors, nurses, portable medical equipment and patients crisscrossed every which way around her.

Betty took a long lungful of oxygen, slowly exhaled and pushed the door open. There was a metallic smell in the closed room. Adrenaline probably. Or maybe, testosterone. Things were happening way too fast. Todd's gold tooth winked. At least that's what she thought she'd seen. She stared at the unfolding picture, it. Todd was sprawled out on a caged bed with various tubes stuck here and there. His face was seamed and his color bad, his freckles standing out on his waxy-white flesh. His mouth groped open, panting. She leaned toward him, saying his name, and firmly but gently took one shoulder to jostle him awake. He slapped at her, then his eyes sprang open, and he stared at her without recognition. He gazed upward with complete, blind horror, and she knew in those first few moments he didn't comprehend the situation.

"Todd," she said again. "Shh, you're all right. You're all right now."

The fog cleared from his eyes. His body clenched rigid, then sagged as the tension left. He gasped. Betty brushed back some hair that was stuck to his sweaty forehead and was appalled at the heat coming off of him. He told Betty, "Thirsty, so thirsty. Find me a soda."

She hesitated, knowing the nurse wouldn't allow him a drink. Instead she stammered, "What happened?"

He laughed, "I bet Mosley is madder than a bunch of wet wasps."

Completely lost in thought she nodded. It seemed she was doing a lot of nodding lately, and nothing was seemingly falling into place. The outcome appeared sinful, a countryside entrance to Hell.

"We can call this our first date Betty," Todd said. It was a moment before the statement seemed to register with Betty. Her eyelashes fluttered rapidly, and for a moment she was staring at him with unmistakable confusion. She returned a baffled glare and thought he's apparently, out of his mind. At least she thought so. He wasn't out of his mind; he was delirious, surrounded by the attention he'd been craving. Drooling, he looked up at the group of women neighboring his bed. Betty was rushed out of his room and she watched as the nurses peeled his clothes off, piled ice packs on his body. He lay listless on the hospital frame; his head swelling into bumps across his head. He convulsed, the nurses rolled him to his side, and the charge nurse popped a long needle into his backside. When he tilted left, he fell back, thudding the bed. They removed the ice and buried him in broad layers of heated blankets. Betty overheard the discussion. The staff was instructed to ice and heat every fifteen minutes.

There's nothing else that you -- "He was asleep. His chest was moving in and out steadily, his breathing deep. She'd been warned he was sedated and the visit would have to be short. Babbs wanted to tell the nurse she wasn't in that big of a hurry, but she kept that particular news flash to herself. In his medicated state Todd's gold tooth glittered again. Pity and a type of motherly instinct tore her; after all, he was just a big lug. She turned on her heel and walked out of the room. Betty thought about his eyes. They were emotional, not like when she first met him. She thought of how little emotion he'd showed when they first met. Maybe this should have been a warning sign.

Babbs collapsed against the pane of the hospital room and her knees buckled, legs wobbled, and she heard the inappropriate sentences spurt from Todd's mouth. She could taste gray sludge on her tongue; the newness of seeing pain from surface level, and in steady rhythms her breathing subsided to a more normal pace. She felt a push from behind; it was Steve.

"Everything okay?" he inquired.

Betty didn't speak for a long time, her back to him. He

studied the curve of her back. At last she said, "No idea, he's out of his mind."

"Well, that's nothing new, he'll be okay. We need to get back to the Chinese house and see if they witnessed what actually happened. The state patrol won't give the paper any details." He held her gaze. Steve helped Betty for a split second, and then side-stepped, shot her forward toward the exit and picked up the cell, called Tiny Blalock to the hospital to retrieve the company truck from the curb. He knew she was in no shape to drive.

Babbs slammed into his car, felt what seemed quarts of fluid spraying from her mouth. She'd actually vomited.

"Just horrific!" yelled Steve. She didn't know if he was talking about her or Todd. He reminded her of a hippo trying to balance a beam. Cooley left her with the impression of comparing Todd to a dog that had an accident and his nose pushed into the poop.

Betty looked up at his impressionable eyes, questioned what in the world he was rambling on and on about. Fall's steam and a bad odor rose from the pavement of Hospital Drive.

Back at the scene of the accident they spotted the same crowd still lingering after the crash. The nightly news's crew was there, getting the scoop from the Chinese people who'd witnessed the entire incident. Todd had been stuffing a breakfast burrito filled with a hotdog into his mouth when three deer ran out in front of him. His bug slammed sideways, rolled, and tumbled into the soybean field. No one but him was involved in the crash. And he had been wearing his seat belt. There was nothing much else to report.

Cooley drove Babbs to her lake house, offered to wait in the car so she could shower, clean up and comb her disgruntled hair. She asked him to come in and make a pot of coffee so they could have some caffeine. Steve looked around at her place. It wasn't formal or forbidding. The couch and the kitchen table chairs called out a welcome. It gave him a few minutes to catch his breath, and for an instant he wanted to tell her he was sorry for Todd, but he shied from the explanation she might want. He was out of practice at apologies and hated explanations. She dripped out of the shower in record time, and they were back on the road in less than fifteen minutes.

Steve remarked about the off-the-wall comments the trooper had made, informed Betty that the officer had stated he'd have thrown Todd in the cooler if he wasn't so disoriented from the accident for driving distracted. First time she'd heard of that ticket. But of course, she figured she would hear about a lot more in this county than she had anticipated. It certainly wasn't going to be boring if one would gauge her first month of work compared to what had happened thus far.

Babbs had an uncanny ability to size up moments in a matter of seconds. She'd already seen a lot of things in her short lifetime. She remembered when she was five and how she'd seen a green snake dangling like moss in a tree in Mississippi. Betty had tried to point it out to her mother who claimed she was seeing things. Each summer they'd lived there she watched for the snake.

Then there was last year when she traveled back home,

bought a lottery ticket and picked numbers randomly on four of the slots and on the fifth slot a slew of numbers popped in her head. She colored the dots and that night four of the numbers was picked. Unfortunately, the powerball number wasn't one of them. But it was $150.00 nonetheless. Her grandpa once told her, "Girlie, you've got the sight — you're going to see things others can't."

She thought again about Todd and promised not to speculate about anyone anymore. If he pulled through she planned to give him a new beginning, maybe even invite him to Northwoods Baptist.

Steve pulled into the gas station to refuel and she flipped the mirror down, smoothed her flattened hair and stared at the face staring back, her own.

Cooley's mind was fixed somewhere else and they cruised toward Norwood. He'd bought her a Coke to settle her stomach and she didn't feel the need for a nerve pill anymore.

"Is it always this frantic when you're working Steve?" she asked. He looked at her doe face and smiled. She kept thinking of things she could say to start the conversation back, but was at a loss of words.

All she wanted to do was take her hard felt feelings toward Todd back, inhale a deep breath and wish this were just a dream.

Betty stared out the car window, the late morning sun caught her cheeks and silhouetted her face. Her Indian looks slanted the day. Fog slowly hung in sheets, lifting golden where it caught the sun. She had never thought of the world as a particularly safe place.

It was one of those blistering hot afternoons that North Carolinians learn to endure. As the afternoon broiled they seemed to be the only life moving on the back road. In the cauldron-like heat, Betty looked up at Steve, and said she'd pray, "That hundreds of angels would weep crocodile tears and cool this place off." Her wish wasn't granted. If anything, the already fiery hot day was heating up dangerously in another part of the town, only six miles away.

Back at the office Bernard Bakes met her in the conference room, offered her a warm cup of black coffee. She awkwardly thanked him, confused for a second.

He said, "It's been a humdinger of a month for you. Do you still feel like a new hire?" Bakes didn't even wait for her answer, it was quitting time and he expressed the thoughts for a better weekend.

All Betty could think about was climbing into her car, putting it on automatic cruise and steering toward her address. The sign outside her new home, placed at the base of a stone row, pebbled white read "Gate to Lake Tillery." In the fading light, the shadows of softly swaying pine trees along the driveway printed a golden barcode crossing the newly sprung grass. The countless stars newly appearing above the house twinkled. At home she hauled out her laptop and banged out an e-mail to her folks. She wouldn't be visiting this weekend, too much excitement. She read it, nodded satisfaction and pressed the send button.

The bay window reflected her outline as she plumped

the cushion and positioned herself for an evening to watch the ducks and contemplate. Betty had completely forgotten her dinner date with Gary — had only thirty minutes to transform herself into a glittery person for the night. He'd been out of town on assignment and had no clue as to the day's activities. She just wanted to put all these thoughts to bed, pulled out several dresses and pumps, making quick choices before his arrival.

Gary cruised the quiet street toward Betty's house, thinking she might have completely forgotten their plans. She hadn't answered her cell. But he figured that might be something to be expected.

Farmland had once surrounded Babbs's Lake Tillery home like a green sea. Milk cows could still be seen oozing dung, drifting toward brim beds dense with rainbow color. The land had been subdivided into lake lots. Huge waterfront houses went up on two-acre lots, big piers sprouted in and out of the water. These houses were mostly tourist weekend stays that rumbled in from every direction. The owner's names were scripted in wood, plotted with pansies. Sleep deprived alcoholics spaced the porches out, and as they listened to country songs of love gone wrong the sky tinted them blue. Gary wondered why and how Betty Babbs had found this community.

9 – NEW ASSIGNMENT

A silent crowd assembled in the newsroom, clumped like human droplets. Betty thought everyone was waiting, always waiting. Outside the room secretaries and clerks filled the air with fast talk. The maintenance men passed through world-weary looks.

Mitch Mosley was motioning the regular staff back to work and the night floaters to head on home. Todd was yesterday's news.

"Morning Betty," her boss nodded. She addressed his greeting, smiled and entered the meeting.

Stela removed a bobby pin from her hair, fastening the blonde streaks more securely. Her eyes were wide-set, long-lashed, and fixated on the men. Metro enjoyed saying things that held double meanings or asking riddles. Beneath the softness, Betty felt the intensity, the gritty terrain of her questioning mind. She was the type of woman that could swing a pendulum that would hypnotize you and ask questions and tell if you're lying by the way it swings back and forth.

Steve stared at Stela for a moment, and then turned to eye-catch Betty.

Goldie Beckett placed her hands on her hips. She was flamboyant, just not to the degree of Stela. Her hair was shorter and not blond streaked. She dressed more soberly, was quieter, an almost colorless girl compared to Stela, a spinning top. Stela was a number of records stacked on the automatic changer, but Goldie walked with a delicious rhythm and a hip swing of grace. Her smile was soft and she loved to show off her long legs, worked her shoulders a little more when the men were around. She was a beautiful, delicate, and sensitive woman who treasured literature, art, and all things beautiful. She wrote poetry, was a brilliant piano layer and read at least one lust-curdling novel a week. She started to say something but Steve touched her arm and said, "Why don't we just listen?"

Cookie Metstrom's face was turned to one side; her rosebud mouth, red and parted. Buttermilk skin, chubby cheeks, and pug nosed balanced her black cat eye shaped glasses. Her hair was sleek, pageboy straight and barely brushed her neck. Five five, trim figure, slightly long-waisted, eyes a pale bloodshot. No make up, scrubbed complexion. A girly woman. Twenty-eight but she could have easily been mistaken for a college student. Babbs thought if anyone looked like a porcelain doll it was Cookie.

All three girls listened to the guys talk about Betty before the meeting with envy. Goldie said, "Always keep your competition closer to your heart than your friends. At least I'm exactly as I am on paper. I betray lovers as ruthlessly as men have always betrayed women and I'd only break a man's heart, shattering it into so many pieces they'd never be able to put it together again. Girls, I want a string of diamonds, big as ostrich eggs, matching the size of my man's testicles."

Cookie said, "I thought that was your enemies."

"Whatever?" answered Stela.

Mitch Mosley had overheard the innocent chatter and thought life would be more fun with Betty Babbs around. According to Gary, she would make a perfect food critic. He'd nonchalantly shared his breakfast with Mitch. Both got a good laugh out of it. With Todd's mishap he couldn't think of a better replacement and thought how he hadn't had the opportunity to ask Todd where he found that delicious cake. He would have sprung for one to bring up the office atmosphere.

Who knew Albemarle might even get a skyscraper or two. After all, he'd convinced Betty Babbs to work for him!

Turning back to the group Mitch ran his hands down his shirt, hurriedly, as if searching for unfastened buttons. Today his clothes were simple – plaid cotton over khaki pants and tennis shoes. Pausing for a moment he looked at each one of them and stopped at Betty's face. "Well Babbs here's your chance. You are going to be our temporary food critic, until Todd can resume his job. Same as before, I'll be sending you on the assignments and hope you'll have the good sense to be where I send you."

Feeling as if she was under the spotlight delicate lavender veins lifted her eyes to his and nodded. Like a hummingbird zeroing in on a red plastic sugar-water feeder, the thought struck her of how ironic this situation was.

Steve Cooley was assigned the task of visiting the Chinese onlookers that might have witnessed Todd's entire accident. Betty recalled them as being the same restaurant owners Todd had ticked off with his comment about things being tossed out the back door. Naturally, Mosley thought it would be a good idea for Babbs to tag along, especially, since he planned on her doing an excellent review on their restaurant in the near future.

Two hours later she found herself and Steve looking into the face of an ancient man. She felt her face cradled in the chilly gaze of his pale black and white eyes and the almost angry set off his thin, colorless lips. His heels rocked back and forth on his little screened-in-porch, watching her like a cottonmouth in two feet of muddy water. He had deep eyes, glassy as water. He didn't smile, and he didn't talk. Betty's chest was stuck in an airless place. Her pulse was jacked and she felt weak and shaky on her feet.

Within minutes of their arrival his wife, Chin Lui, poked her head out of the front door. "You the reporters that called before?" They both replied they were. "Chang, invite our company in."

Chang motioned them in stating, "Finding the faith is what folks call being reborn." Steve and Betty looked at each other, thinking maybe this was a Chinese proverb.

Chang continued, "Where we come from the ancients believe that everything or anything people need already exists. We moved to Lake Tillery to begin our dream and raise a perfect family. Maybe, make a little extra to send back home. But Chin Lui's sesame chicken is one of the things that have allowed us to be prosperous. Right now,

I'm too tired to share the recipe but if you come back again later... Where was I?"

Babbs asked her question once more, "Did you see the accident?"

"Not entirely, but I woke up to something that sounded like Derby Night at the County Fair. Then screams of sirens sounded. Chin Lui is my wife and the only woman that puts sesame on my chicken. Out in the front on the main road was a sight I'd never seen before. Strings of traffic tied together like kites stuck in mid air. It was that lime-green Volkswagen that both of us immediately recognized. Just a big mess, like a circus in my front yard. Damn invasion of privacy. All I wanted to do was resume my nap.

But it was that fat red headed guy from the paper and wouldn't you know he'd be choking on a dog. I figured it was a drunk driver by the way he'd rolled that car. His face is going to have wrinkles like push down socks if he keeps cramming his mouth with junk and spouting it as well."

As Steve joined in and they all talked, the air cleared. Chin Lui poured us a cup of hot tea. "Weak as water," Chang Lui spat. And Betty didn't think he was referring to his wife's tea. The afternoon ended with pleasant feelings and a promise of a free lunch. Something they'd both share with Mitch Mosley.

Sunday was fast approaching and the sermon was "Gospel Brings About Eternity," the preacher being a newly ordained minister by the name of Tony Roman. Betty substituted gospel for gossip.

Saturday was lonesome, so she decided to take a drive,

traveling in a totally opposite direction from what was originally planned, driving downtown near Anson Avenue where the Episcopalian Church was loud with music, amen's, laughing, shouting, and the building nearly rocking off its foundation.

Her car pivoted into the parking lot, and like a depraved person she snuck to the panes, and peered in. It was not like any congregation she'd ever seen. There were guitar players, drummers, and even a fiddler. Her mind lingered toward the song, "The Devil's Gone Down to Georgia," or something like that. The whole church was wobbling like Moses and his animals must have in the great flood.

Up front Stela, Cookie, and Goldie were all singing and writhing with the music. She had to admit even the spirit moved her. Warm and welcome her heart drifted with the chorus, and urged her legs inside. The three girls jumped to their feet, effusive in their greetings. They motioned Babbs to sit with them.

On the step up platform in front of the podium stood Tiny Blalock in his trademark khakis, hat, and horn rimmed glasses pulling his guitar strings. She focused on how relaxed he was, looking very much like a latter-day Jesus. His fingertips were cherry red and up close his blue eyes sparkled when he played. The sound of it gave Betty a prickle of pleasure, like listening to the Grand Ole Opry on her grandfather's radio. She felt the goose bumps on her forearms and across the back of her spine. She thought the music was similar to wandering orphans, children that always tried to find a home. The tunes sounded nostalgic and old-fashioned, like something off an old Gospel record, mournful and sweet at the same time, Betty thought to herself, "He can play a guitar, but can't sing." Babbs thought this was the prettiest music that she'd ever heard. She just wanted to holler and jump up and down and couldn't sit still on that pew bench when the tunes started snaking around the church. No wonder so many were letting their hair down, yelling and leaping off those benches, commencing to dance and clog around. With everybody whooping and laughing every time he touched the strings hell broke loose in that gathering. This flatfooting, foot dragging, sliding eccentric lifestyle peppered the church with hot licks.

Betty thought she couldn't believe she came out of the hills and landed in the country of churches and singles. Work was fun and her parents would be proud if they knew how often she was visiting church. Mama believed in everything, but Daddy was skeptical. He used to say the Bible was all bunk. He was raised Pentecostal, but she believed he was a true spiritualist, which is how he raised her. He probably knew or had his speculations about her church going. Mamma's heart would have popped out of her chest if she thought there might be another ulterior motive.

When Betty was ten she was baptized in the Chatta-hoochee River. First warm Sunday in June. A spirit-filled line guarded the banks. Everybody was spouting glory and amen's. That water was so cold and she remembered how she cried out, "Oh Lord."

Her mother hushed her mouth, and told her to believe. Religion is a living faith in Macon County. Mamma was sanctified and determined that all of her children would remain within the folds of church, out of the clutches of the Devil. She thought back about Saturday's prayer meeting and realized Lake Tillery had raised a lot of lost souls.

10 - WEATHER CHANGES

On Wednesday morning, forty-six minutes later after the morning assignment, Babbs emerged breathless, her mind flipping cartwheels regarding new ideas for Todd's critiquing column. She had already started jotting notes, even during interrupted sleep. The column was dull. In time Betty felt she could influence Mr. Mosley in a new direction even Todd would like.

Her heart and stomach did a simultaneous stutter step when she found out she was assigned to the Chinese restaurant again. Upon entering she looked at the neon Chinese character on the restaurant's check out counter. A black eel in the aquarium in front of her batted his head against the glass as if trying to get her attention and say something like, "Hey, Babbs, why don't you just run screaming out of the restaurant? Don't stop until you get to Broughton State Hospital."

The young girl seated her and invited her to eat from the buffet for free today. After she ate her free dinner at Chin and Chang's the night before ideas sprouted like well-watered weeds. Chin taught Betty the secret of Chinese sponge cake. The cook had placed a lace doily on the cake's top surface and sprinkled powdered sugar over it. Ms. Lui also shared that on special occasions she used colored powder. Babbs asked Chin if she could share that tidbit with her readers, and she readily consented. She also shared Mrs. Lui's other advise of how the cake would fall if too little flower was used, and also how it would rise in the center and crack if too much flour was used.

Betty was not a great cook with the exception of her "Better Than Sex cake", but as willing as her readers to try and learn.

Tom Martin happened to be passing The Heart of Stanly Motel when he witnessed an unbelievable scene. As always his camera was poised next to him. Two Mexican workers had been cleaning rooms when they'd discovered a huge boa underneath a table, slouched under the bed and touching the bathroom floor.

Martin was a tall, slim boy, with light pasty skin and a smile that displayed marvelous teeth. Just as he could argue for hours, with intellectual substance, about any type of subject, he was also capable of becoming involved in passionate dialogues on literature, art or sports, especially football, and the feats of the local high school team. There was something in his character that communicated enthusiasm, idealism, generosity, and the rugged sense of religion that guided his life. All of these traits threw him into coordination of the calamity.

One of the women, very fluent in Spanish, screamed, called for the Virgin Mary to appear.

Her rosary rolled tight tiny fists that flayed upwards.

The other woman, huge breasted with jiggly rotund thighs that were excitedly dancing up and down in tune to the fever of the moment hovered close.

Tom knew what to do and swung into action. He started texting Steve with no success, then the office. Realizing this could be Thursday's front page he struck a similar pose as one of the women. Frozen to the rail banister, his mouth O-My-God shaped, his fingers awkwardly opened the shutter and started wildly snapping. A reeled back snake startled from the flashing light hissed a desperate grin. He thought this snake had to be at least fifteen feet and at least ten inches round. A crowd was gathering in the lower parking lot. His recorder caught the precarious whispers, gossip, and awed moments.

A big-busted girl with bleached hair, obviously intoxicated, was fast approaching, displaying pyramids of tattoos, and darting a snaggle-toothed smile. She marched into the room demanding everyone to leave. Her vulgar manners shocked Betty. The girl was country-fried stupid, not to mention in need of some enhanced psychiatric drugs.

It wasn't quite checkout time. The owner, Mr. Patina, a gentleman from Shrilanka, dark and rather attractive, entered the scene powered by repulsive-sounding gasps. He'd risen as if from the grave with a tropical suddenness. His flashy shirt and silk pants flashed inside the room. Flaming torches glowed from the wallpaper hung over the wrong-sized furniture, and the bed covers spilled onto the floor inches from Oliver. Apparently, the young girl, named Deborah, Debbie to her friends, howled the snake's name Oliver in repetition. She was moving her mouth, like she was talking to someone, only no one was there, and no one could hear any words coming out of her.

What a twister this press release would be and Tom Martin had the best shots. Cooley finally appeared as if the wind had tunneled him through the traffic jam of people in the parking lot. Wearing an olive suit and yellow shirt, open collared Betty's tempted to give him a wink – just a little one. But she doesn't do it. "Tom?" she asks. He doesn't hear her. He's so wrapped up in the scene he doesn't even notice she's stepped back. He's getting closer, and maybe because of what's happening, her skin begins to crawl. Steve stared for a moment, then nodded and went to the motel door. He opened it half a foot and peeked in. The sun had shifted or moved behind a cloud, and the entrance was in a cool shadow. Anxious to get the scoop he removed his jacket, looked at Tom and explained how he'd come from a long fiery line of Pentecostal ministers with a penchant for snake handling and how his dad had focused groups with his handler abilities. Tom wasn't surprised. Debbie hadn't fed Oliver. That was the main problem.

A proper conversation was not appropriate for this moment as Oliver squeezed his master. Debbie nervously spouted how she was tired of nipple rings and stretch pants and motel rooms, how she'd been faking the scene and how she needed to be a solo act from now on.

A dramatic event. Debbie stilled and her boyfriend joined the action swinging a twelve-pack.

Steve went inside, coaxed the snake to release the drunken woman. With one hand on the boa's head and the other gripping its backside he pushed and pulled the boa away from Debbie. He didn't look up from his work.

He performed this act of affection gently as one would do with a baby. Then he began talking to the snake in a soft voice.

"Can I try to help?" Tom questioned.

"Just hold him here and push forward like this," Steve said.

Her boyfriend sputtered, "Who'd ever thought?" All eyes turned on him. An older man obsessed with a wired young woman. Hunger spilled from their eyes and Tom kept snapping. The best picture was of Steve's rear side coaxing the snake from a squeezing position.

There was an extremely charged stillness before the police and animal control arrived. Guests were lining the office door to turn in their key cards and collect their ten-buck deposit. Albemarle didn't have that many motel accommodations and the tourists were anxious to move on.

Martin listened and nodded as the scene rolled on like a movie. The group parted like the Red Sea for Steve and Tom.

"What a morning!" was all Steve offered.

Tom said, "You got that right!"

Cooley turned back to the dissipating crowd, smoothed the wrinkles from his tossed jacket and moistened his upturned lips. Tom hovered his elbow, passed the recorded tape, and both agreed the office was definitely the place to go. Content with the morning battle, they tossed their jackets over their shoulders, and began punching each other's shoulder, saying to each other, "Who's the man?" Both resumed their dignified exit.

"Let's go to Tiendos," Tom said. "I'm buying."

"Okay," Cooley tuned in. "I'm hungry."

Meanwhile, Betty was sipping a hot Apple Cider twister from the Come Back Café and eating a sandwich she'd picked up there on the outside deck. It tasted like the Saran Wrap it had been wrapped in. Good thing she wasn't reviewing the diner. She felt a hand on her arm and alarms sounded. Leo Sparks, a weather reporter for Channel 9, had made the languid move.

"Betty Babbs?" he questioned.

"Yes?" she responded.

"May I join you?" He extended his hand and she shook it as she looked into his face.

"Certainly," she spoke. After his forward move Betty quickly glanced at his ring finger. No ring and his fingers were totally tanned. They sat outside, on the terrace. It was a warm afternoon, with few clouds, and all of Albemarle seemed to have poured out onto the street enjoy the good weather. He ordered an apple cider and smiled at her.

She laughed a deep throaty gurgle, and consciously applauded her new position. Babbs could hardly breathe and small hairs were raising her arms and shoulders. Leo Sparks presented his overactive magnetism and recognized the symptoms of attraction.

Her cell on vibrate jiggled her mind. Excusing herself she answered. "Be right there," she stated.

After an apology to Leo of having to quickly leave she opened her car door and the vehicle rappelled into autopilot. Betty kicked off her low pumps, relieving the developing blister.

She envisioned Leo, the weather man, dressed in nothing but a raincoat, with an umbrella for a pointer, rain boots, alternating between the different areas, sweating over the weather map while her small hands with their delicate fingers struggled to open his umbrella, and speaking into his ear with that slow, sensual southern voice of people from the mountains. She'd never believed in love at first sight, especially with a weatherman.

"Don't be crazy," she whispered to herself. At the office she jumped up to her laptop and pecked out a review any restaurateur would revel in.

Mitch had called all the staff in, and the snakes all slinked out. It was a hopeless morning and she felt jet-lagged from driving in all directions. She sat up, felt the phone's vibration and urgently answered the wireless jingle. "It's Leo," the voice murmured. "Enjoyed what lunch we shared and would like to be able to see you again."

Betty invited him to church that night and promised a home cooked meal. Who could turn that down? Being the latest correspondent hired she desperately wanted acceptance.

"Sure, why not, but we'll visit my church?" he answered.

"Oh, okay," she replied. "Where do you attend?"

He answered "The Church of the Nazarene." Another

new hangout Betty thought. Maybe Stanly County had much more to offer than a cruise liner of singles mingling. "Sure, see you around 6:00 tonight," and she slowly closed her cell. Four days to go to Sunday and hump day was going out in happiness with the thought of tonight's church date.

She e-mailed her story to Mitch, picked up her pocketbook and headed home. On the way home, she stared out the window at a line of people stretching out the door of a small ice cream shop. That looked like fun. Possibly another story line.

Leo was doing his best to act casual about Wednesday's church service. However strange, Leo was one of the few people she'd met in Stanly County that made her feel truly comfortable. Reminded her of her brother back home. Why was it the guys she liked were good-looking and smooth like Gary and Steve, knowing all the while they were married only to their jobs?

It wasn't any cooler outside the church, but the air was fresh. The crickets were loud as the pause in the darkness. Time passed quietly as if in a dream, Betty thought later. They nodded and laughed.

He left her with the night and his footsteps behind her sounded across the sidewalk. Then he was back, plopped hip-to-hip.

"You know a woman, especially one named Babbs, deserves a showstopper at least one time in their life," he casually stated. Once things seem settled she shrugged his comment off and said, "Only for love. Then, and only then."

"Whatever," he said.

"Yeah."

"But you don't even have a boyfriend Betty?"

She shrugged in harmony. "Not ready to commit, I'm young. Why is everyone worried about my relationships?"

"Some people think when you turn twenty five, you're an old maid."

"Hah," she laughed.

He'd caught her completely off track. Neither of them said anything for the longest time. Then he said, "Better say goodnight."

"I'll see you tomorrow," she responded. Betty should have gone to bed, but sat a little longer lost in the stars.

11 - NEW DIRECTIONS

Betty was astonished to find two vases filled with roses the next morning at work. There was a note, promises of a wild dining opportunity with instructions to wear a Sunday frock, and be ready to go at lunch. The note was not signed. She became fascinated and intrigued at the same time, realizing she'd chosen the perfect time to wear her new red dress.

Stela called out, "Your devoted slave is calling again. Can I tell him not to tie the line up too long? Mosley's gone crazy with the telephone log. Wants us to be more time efficient. Besides that didn't the boss want you to check out The Brown Derby for lunch today?" Cookie looked back, said, "Jeez she forgot." "No, just running late," Betty emphasized.

It didn't take long to realize the invitation was from Leo for an innocent lunch. They met on Main Street, parked side-by-side and entered the front door, which was smack in the middle of the building.

Strangers nodded hello. Leo pulled Betty's chair out,

waited on the waitress, silverware and water. Then he quietly asked her to join him in bowing their heads in thanksgiving. The chef's line stretched clear across the restaurant. The customer could watch the complete process of his or her lunch being prepared. One star up for the restaurant. The waitress hung tight to the tables refilling the drinks, seemingly, after a few sups were taken. Two stars up and counting. The cook grinned and delivered our liver and onions doused in gravy to the table. The waitress trailed, carrying the sides and condiments. Three stars up for sure.

For a while they sipped their drinks in silence. Her roll was on the table, untouched, and Leo, bent on making jokes, said that since something apparently was taking away my appetite, he'd make the sacrifice and take care of the crusty half moon. Leo suspected Babbs was using her mental calculator to grade the service.

"Dessert?" the waitress asked.

"Gracious no, I'm full, how about you Leo?" Betty said.

"None for me," and Leo patted his tight abs, nodding in agreement.

They both reached for the tab, but as Babbs did with all her guests she invited to lunch pulled the company credit card, flipped it out and signed the ticket. Definitely, a four star up performance.

Leo scanned the waitress and a silly smile exploded across his face. Five stars for Babbs. "Next time we'll have to stick to the low-cholesterol menu." Conversation ended in the parking lot and Sparks said, "Call ya." Betty started to throw in about talking after work, but decided not to spoil the moment. Mitch would just have to get over it.

Back at the office Goldie elbowed the star food critic. "Well, we want details! Is he the sleek canary that whisks you away into the night? After all, you're the girl with bee-stung lips and wear the perfume that evokes fields of gardenias. Even wear your blonde hair studded back with hot pink pearls. All you need is a glittery rose tattooed on your chest to sparkle in the night. We all know you're a garden in slow bloom and I believe that you lead an electric life. Is he high voltage girlfriend?"

Betty smiled a similar silly smile to Leo's. "Just a job, eat and learn." By this time she was half convinced the entire religious community was wacko. With the afternoon splitting fast everyone exited the building around five. A fire drill couldn't have gone off any better.

Back home Betty walked the line of her property, discovered a log that could fit two nicely. She thought her own private love log. She sat, brushed her toes between blades of pine needles, and rested her shoulder against the main trunk. Soon her eyes drifted shut and her arms drooped, her body stirred the cool breeze. Fifteen minutes later, her brain rested, she yawned backwards, looked at the beautiful red sunset, ripples of

dark blue water and thought of how life didn't get much better than this.

At approximately the time this thought occurred something plopped white/gray on her forehead. She saw the sea gull spread its wings in flight and cried, "Yuck, oh no." Sure enough -- poop was dripping down the edge of her nose. It was without a doubt time to go inside and get ready for bed. She used the bottom of her flannel to wipe the goop. She wondered if Nazarene women would have had the same thoughts she did. "Truce?" she spoke to the sky, the sea gull long out of sight.

12 - NEW INVITATIONS

Tiny Blalock escorted Betty into the building the next morning. He was grateful for the sting of air on his face and the way each inhalation sent a stunned tingle through his lungs. This was real. In a slow-get-to-know-you walk he mentioned that Gary had revealed going to church with her. She waited for him to speak again. "Gary tells me you're a mountain girl. So, does that mean you're an Honest-to-God hillbilly?" "Lol," Betty laughed. "No more like a flatbilly." Tiny's eyebrows arched. "Well one leg is not longer than the other, and I love the flat land. So call me a flatbilly." He glanced at the hem of her pale indigo suit, thinking of how it accented her eye color.

"I was wondering?" he sputtered. "Would you like to visit my church Sunday?" Taken back Babbs didn't answer immediately, just stared at the blue clouds for a moment and said, "Sure, why not? Where do you attend?" He dragged his shoe in the gravel. Sunshine winced his eyes. "Norwood Pentecostal."

She smiled thinking about how she'd made the rounds. Must be similar to how a minister visited in the old west.

Times weren't that much different, just people and the places.

"So happens we're having a pot luck dinner after the sermon. It would give you a chance to meet some more singles in town," Blalock offered.

Tiny shook his head in incredulity, not believing she'd actually accepted. Things were looking brighter for him. Maybe, even a life-changing moment. She had always thought of Tiny as animated and eager to please. His long curly hair made him appear more distinguished even though he wore glasses. They didn't detract from his raw masculinity.

Betty's mind had jumped ahead to Sunday, sharing the gospel with new folks, children chasing children, and eating a lot of weird food. Something she had to decide regarding what her dish would be. One thing for sure it wouldn't be green bean casserole. Just two-days-and-a-half away.

She'd have to get her cookbooks out of the basement and play with the recipes, maybe make something from scratch.

Her pace slowed as she entered the foyer to the reporter's room, and thought of how odd it was that her career and personal life crossed. So many possibilities. Gary hinted at a date for church Sunday, but Betty explained she'd already made other plans. "Compared to you Babbs, my life is dull."

It was almost lunchtime and there was an awkward moment. Mosley was fired like a lit match. He gathered the staff like kindling, sending everyone out in a flurry of flight.

Steve had been sent to cover a text-messaging threat at two local schools, one that locals took seriously since troubles such as this had risen to alarming levels across the country. Gary was to check out the suspension of a teacher involved in a teenage sex scandal. Tom Martin was expected to be in two places at the same time.

Betty helloed, "Good luck with that."

Stela, Cookie and Goldie were assigned the task of straightening out the classifieds from the personals. Somehow when the last group was sent to type they were mixed together causing the phones to ring off their hooks. Tiny was on standby. Bernard Bakes had to travel to an out of town 2A high school to get the scoop on their stats for Friday night's football game.

Babbs's assignment was a Subway in Albemarle. Mr. Mosley had her doing rating checks for the public. She hated checking the percentage score DHEC awarded before ordering. At least her figure remained intact. And Leo hadn't called. The remainder of the week progressed in this fashion.

Betty took a huge bite of her sub and heard a voice say, "Excuse me ma'am? Is this seat taken?"

Mouth stuffed with turkey, lettuce, onions and tomato she looked up into Leo's face. Betty struggled to swallow and flagged him to join her.

"What's a nice guy like you doing in a place like this? You are following me?"

Sparks smiled, put his food down and pulled the chair out to seat himself. Even though he was merely pulling a chair away from a table, he did it with all the style of Simon, the guy that made rock stars.

He was practically leering at her. Or maybe, he had a natural leer. Well maybe he did, but there was small sparks between them. She was hoping he'd invite her to visit his church again. Well, Hell would probably freeze over first.

13 - POT LUCK

Saturday the cookbooks were confiscated from the basement. So many choice dishes, but Babbs was well aware of her limited cooking skills. She debated about bringing two dishes; maybe goo-goo clusters, barbequed baked beans, even chicken, but settled on a simple dish of Jerusalem artichokes and her infamous cake. Back home her mamma called them sunshokes, and about all you had to do was use a vegetable peeler, then boil, fry or serve sautéed. She decided fried in olive oil would be best. They were nutty, sweetly flavored and crunchy. Something someone else probably wouldn't bring. One of those weird dishes.

With that settled and prepared Betty decided to stretch out, read or nap. The cell rang. "So much for that thought," she mumbled. "God surely directs my life." It was just Tiny confirming tomorrow's church date and making sure her directions to where the church was located was clear. They planned on meeting at 9:30 a.m., the Sunday school service at 9:45 a.m., with morning sermon beginning at

11:00 a.m. Covered dish would start at 12:15 p.m. Her life was mapped out.

The Norwood Pentecostal Church was located in the leafy suburbs of town, and when Babbs walked inside a nice lady mouthed attendance was of the utmost importance. Betty had a lingering feeling that visiting there was going to be similar to an orgy in a graveyard. Tiny had her striding along in an upright way that he held, as though they were on their way to an urgent meeting.

The church was a long roughly timbered structure with few windows and the rooms turned out to be big as a bowling alley when you stepped in. The poor preacher was a middle-aged woman with hair that flew in all directions. She greeted them heartedly.

Tiny related to God the way he did his absent father, one who'd run out when he was born, but still remotely remained in the picture.

His dad would send a card and a check every blue moon, and write expectations in the reference area. On every check and card were ridiculous demands: "And remember son, thou shalt not dishonor they father or mother. Affectionately, Dad." It was outrageous he'd ask anything of him. But he'd always tried to commit to his father's wishes, or disobeying him at the cost of seething guilt. It's just the fact Tiny kept hoping that if he'd do the right thing long enough his dad would finally show up. He thought a sucker is born every minute.

This very old lady who was so frail that her neck could barely support the burden of her elderly head began to laugh. It was a terrible sound, like very brittle paper being shredded into tiny pieces. She tells Betty the preacher is speaking in tongues. She was more than shocked and gazed around at the children, adolescents, and grown-ups moving, jumping and cutting figures.

"Think of all the offerings you've got to make to receive the gift," lilted from the old lady's voice.

Babbs was in no position to rhapsodize about the Pentecostal way of life. This moment, thank God, didn't last too long, because some people came to the front of the enormous church and began singing songs and playing assorted musical instruments. The music was bubbly, sounds Betty could have shimmy-shaked to or became entranced like a stoned individual high on drugs.

Tiny yanked her arm, urged her to join in. "Don't be shy," he said. So she let him drag her into the front circle and raised her hands singing joyously.

He added, "Be trouble-free, and relax. You're getting overexcited; we still have the rest of the afternoon, and all that food to eat."

Betty's thinking it's crazy the words that spill out of people's mouths. She was struck how small she was to him, her head barely touching his shoulder. It was a hard feeling to describe. Part of her was appalled at her shameless habit for seeing drama in every conceivable situation.

It wasn't long before they tiptoed out the back door, feeling high on life, and laughing loudly. The food feast was next.

Sunday had started without a hitch; twelve covered corning ware bowls fanned out in perfect symmetry. Eight contained green bean casserole, one honey-baked ham, three squash casseroles, loaf bread, iced tea, perked coffee, soft drinks, plastic plates, spoons, forks, sporks and knives finished the last table along with Betty's Jerusalem artichokes. She guessed someone mistook her main dish for desert. Her surprise "Better Than Sex Cake" sat on a table by itself. Even Tiny didn't see her sneak it in. Someone had provided paper towels, salt and pepper. Not bad for potluck. The minister's husband supplied hot dogs and chips for the children. Taped to the fellowship hall door on a dangling official Church letterhead were directions of how the congregation were to progress.

Young teens had decorated the room and lined the tables together. Surprisingly, there were benches instead of chairs. Tiny brought his and Betty's plate to one of the end tables.

"Do remember that cake Mr. Mosley snatched out of Todd's hand?" asked Tiny.

She bit her lower lip. She had a beautiful bow of a mouth tinted naturally pink. Tiny noticed without wanting o and a peaches and cream complexion that he'd rarely seen on woman once they washed their makeup off. Her hair was a soft, golden blonde. She had swooped it back into a ponytail, but when unfettered, it must reach halfway down her back.

"Yes," she remembered that skit playing out. "Why do you ask?"

"There's another cake sitting on a table by itself that looks just like the one half the staff was trying to gobble down."

She smiled mischievously, hesitated for a minute, glancing at Tiny. Tiny's eyes began to take on a glitter.

"You want believe it but the teen boys disposed of the cake first. Some of the parents are really fussing. I guess one of the girls from the office could have baked it. Saw them earlier."

Babbs didn't own up to baking the cake in addition to the artichoke dish she'd prepared. After drawing a long breath her heart muscles relaxed, but she didn't have the heart to tell him it was her special recipe.

"Sorry we didn't get a piece then. We didn't really need it anyway, with all of the other food."

Playful children turned the switches on and off and homebound housewives chased the little boogers. The faint buzz of chatter hummed the room, and a splotch of sun baked the stained glass. Flies entered in with friends, hovered inches above the plates. Betty swooshed the flies away, and suddenly a shoe smacked the teasing pests, leaving a dull thud ringing in her ears. Tiny had removed his size thirteen shoe, swatted a few more and everyone resumed their meal.

The covered dish dinner was like a party members prepared for, as if they were ascending to heaven. Everything was wonderful and Tiny Blalock acted as if he'd already arrived. Both left transformed.

Betty's phone was ringing when she arrived home. It was Leo. They said their greetings and she explained in detail of how Tiny had murdered a platoon of pests at Sunday's covered dish dinner. Leo and Betty laughed, talked a little longer before bidding goodbyes.

After falling asleep in the lounge chair Betty's eyes adjusted to the rising river. Against a pink sky smudged with orange she admired the woodsy terrain. Two older folks, hands looped, circled the waterfront. They were probably retirees on permanent vacation because they couldn't afford to go anywhere else and really didn't want to. Her land lay between walls of golden wheat; skeins of needle knotted pines and huge red oaks. These trees were crowned with bird nests. The red cardinals and blue jays dotted the skyline. Peace and beauty of her new home stole her soul. Babbs stared up at the heavens and said thanks for such a beautiful day. One she was sure never to forget. A narrow slice of light threw her shadow into deeper thought, a perfect day to dawn steamy, the kind of day in North Carolina where all one should have to do was sit on the deck with a gasping hound dog, drink lemonade and fan yourself into daydreams.

She spoke aloud, "Life's good!"

14 - MORE MISFORTUNE

It was after 9:00 a.m. Monday morning before Betty arrived at the newsroom. Traffic was back-to-back and everyone in view seemed preoccupied. "Morning," from Betty's voice hung above their heads. Paper notebooks tucked under their arm's reach. She watched them for a moment and looked for Mr. Mosley. A note suspended from his office door. Simple instructions for their assignments were to be found on all of their desks. They were all apparently on their own today, and knew what had to be done. Then he noted on the bottom line -- I've gone to take care of an urgent matter.

"Be back soon -- Mitch Mosley."

Soon after lunchtime Mosley returned to work. His disposition was frantic. He called the staff in for a meeting at 2:00 p.m. As he explained to the group his wife had woken up in the middle of the darkness to go to the bathroom, and tripped on a rug. He'd immediately rushed to her side when he heard the loud thump. It hadn't been an hour since they'd gone to bed laughing and smiling. In the next few minutes a strange look took over Mosley's face and his eyes seemed out of control. This couldn't have happened at a worse time. 911 were called and an ambulance dispersed. I remember that within what seemed minutes I was ushered out of the way. The medics had cautiously stabilized her back and neck and ran lights and sirens full blast to the Stanly Hospital. Two hours later he was informed she'd broken her neck, and she was transported to Charlotte Memorial.

Mitch standing in front of the staff was half expecting someone to step forward and say this had to be a terrible mistake, and add a second opinion was a necessity. But a second opinion had been made and a decision to transfer her by helicopter to Charlotte Memorial was immediately made. Their hospital would be better equipped to treat such a serious injury. Besides the type of specialists would be more readily accessible to meet her needs.

The scene described was a slow motion movie that replayed in each person's mind – backward and forward. This was met by a moment of silence. His tone, when he spoke again, was both gently reasonable and apologetic, the tone of a man explaining a harsh truth to a small child. Mitch added he wished he could find some humor in such a serious situation, and his misty eyes brought the sadness of this situation to stark realization.

He softly spoke, "Trouble seems to come in threes, first there was Penelope and Todd, then Peggy, my wife," adding frankly of how he couldn't stomach another deep-seated incident anytime soon. His eyes closed on a wave of pain.

As he peered each of his staff's face they reminded him of beautiful hedges expertly trimmed, the back up coiled hoses that were ready to roll into action, and the office a painting that could be a Norman Rockwell scene. "I'm afraid I'll be away for a small period of time, how long who knows, but in and out, and at this time will delegate new powers to be that will oversee this paper, and hold the responsibility of getting the news out on time. This will not be a distraction that mars this perfect environment. Steve's in charge of assignments, Gary's second in command, Betty's to continue the food critic column and any implementation of new ideas will be acceptable." He explained he would still expect the morning meetings and warned them to expect him unannounced. "Guys, it's a hurry-up-and-wait game."

Babbs stood beneath the buzzing fluorescents, almost willing herself to glance around. Hard stares from this man left her with a realization that expressions were the same ones he'd been accepting all night, looks of loss mixed with turmoil and shock. She was thinking a bomb might have as well had gone off; they all were flailing around looking for some direction, some notion of what to do next. The staff left, their heads nodding in agreement, feeling dressed and undressed. A searing numbness possessed Betty as she thought about Mitch's wife. Dear God, she prayed. Let her be okay. She guessed she must be in shock – like God was taking request from her at this point.

Mosley said, "My heart broke last night, but I'll get through this, just like I know you all will." At this point he exited and Steve stepped up to the plate. He stood at Mitch's desk, frowning, confused. The conversation had taken a leap from one thing to another, without warning, like a needle jumping across a record from one track to the next. Such a contrast between Cooley and the depth of despair that unfolded in a few quick moments, and the ultimate switch of power reminded Betty so much of Anne Sexton, the writer whose poems had always moved her to despair. The remainder of the week was uneventful.

Leo Sparks dropped by her home Friday evening. The knock at the door surprised her and when she opened her door to him she was almost shocked.

"Has something else happened?" was the first words that tumbled out of her mouth.

"No, thank goodness, just worried about you. Betty, you seem depressed. Are you letting these mishaps drown your mood?" He frowned slightly. "Everyone will get through this."

She smiled softly, "It's good to think that." Leo waited, his hands in the pockets of his jean. He looked tired as she felt.

"No Leo, but thanks for asking, don't you want to come in?" Betty thought Leo was handsome in a different way from Gary, a roly-poly southern guy who kind of looked like a young Elvis. But it wasn't in-the-flash, hip-hop way. He was amusing and had an outward personality. Contrast between the two rustled her mind. One steps forward with a surefootedness and profound peace, and the other is learning to live one day at a time – half-heartedly but sincere.

Leo said, "Tomorrow night there's going to be a sock hop at the girl's church." Betty never mentioned she'd already visited, and listened attentively.

"Do you want to go, would be a different pace?" Leo asked.

"Sure, why not." Babbs didn't offer she already knew the pace of this church group.

"Well snap, pick you up at 7:00 p.m. Okay?"

"Great, what are we wearing?"

"The girls said dressy, so dressy it is."

"I'll be ready and thanks for checking on me Leo." He left humming and she started humming.

Leo picked Betty up promptly and they arrived at the fellowship hall on Anson Avenue. Stella was the first to greet them, wearing a red sequined dress, singing, "I'm Gonna Bake Me a Man."

"No, you need to bake one of those "Better Than Sex Cakes" that you won't admit to baking," he retorted to Stella. His eyebrow jerked. It was like talking to himself.

Goldie laid out in a pea-colored green, a color that accentuated her eyes. She watched mutely, thinking about all the single men that didn't live with their mothers. Out of the blue Goldie said, "Teeth are important to me. But that is really none of anyone's business.""

Leo and Betty laughed. They realized she was a little spacey. Cookie dressed in blue that moved with the electric current's air. Babbs thought about the obvious, how each day flowed elevated from slow to groove, and the knowledge that none of them were getting serious or younger. No one escapes taxes, loneliness or death. Everyone really had a blast. The party was exactly what they all needed.

Leaving the party reminded her of leaving church alone,

the drive of a flat two-lane highway, a quiet time that should be lively in the pleats of a beautiful afternoon.

Suddenly, loneliness wrapped arms of loss around her. She missed the rural patchwork of home, the small town Baptists that governed her past, and how few people had ever left the boundaries generations before her had thrived. Leo glanced at Babbs and watched small teardrops spilling. She told him she's thankful to have such good friends and sees the familiar wood plaques planted in posies that she has come to love.

Her mind slips into reverse and thought of what was missing. It was the porches full of flowers; cars covered in dust, school bus children unloading with their books and lunch pails, unwed teenage mothers, work release crews that cut bramble along the mountainside. Even the junky trailers. All these thoughts made her think she was in a prison of sorts. Confined to perfection in such a not-so-perfect world, cosmetically covered with serenity.

They wound up parked at Lake Tillery boat ramp, staring out at the river, the water flecked with diamond scales beneath a high, Carolina-blue sky. Fluffy white clouds, thousands of feet high, crowded the view.

Betty was thinking maybe she needed psychiatric help and made a mental note to talk with Pastor Bob at Northwoods. Maybe Betty needed less visiting privileges and the stability of her own church. She wondered if Leo would go with her. Why was it tragedy touches each person in different ways? Todd's wreck and Mitch's wife's woes.

"We're running out of time," Betty says as Leo pulls into her carport and smiles a crooked grin, not realizing all the conflict she's discovered in her world. She invites Leo in and leaves the needed spiritual discipline on the backburner, thinking maybe she even needed intervention. Using personal days would not be a good idea at this time.

Tuesday posed a reverent head bent over between two desks. Steve's sculptured torso gave her a pause when he rose with his perfect hair. She donned a plastered smile toward Bernard.

"Bakes, what are you doing?" Betty smiled his way and smelled his cologne. Big words, coffee table words followed. This was a stark contrast to his normal conversation.

"Working on my image; Steve suggested this onslaught."

Betty swore, "I'd like nothing better than to believe you, and still have your enthusiasm."

He nodded, observing her with his affectionate, full moon smile. He hesitated for a moment, afraid that what he was going to say might hurt her. It was a question he undoubtedly had been biting his tongue over for a long time. "Is this what you want out of life? Nothing but a job? "

Quipping back at him, "I'd rather ask questions, than answer them." Betty waded away from the discussion, pondered what might possibly be in her future. She thought she needed breakfast and turned to Tom Martin, asking if he had time to join in a stomach feast.

"Okay!" he answered and added, "There's a new breakfast nook in New London.

"Hey, I'm on for it," Betty said. They walked to her car and she clicked the unlock button.

"Shit on a Shingle". It was the first item on the menu. Tom told the waitress that was what he wanted. He tossed words at her, "Their beef chips in gravy over bread will melt in your mouth."

"The title of the dish isn't very receptive, but if it's your recommendation, that'll be breakfast today." She added, "O.J. and coffee, side water." Any type of blend you could desire was on the menu, even latte. She asked for the house blend.

They sat for half the morning, telling old stories, eating the chipped breakfast and drank the strong roasted house blend. Halfway through breakfast they were both ready to sprawl out and nap.

"Two much food! Does this mean a good review?" questioned Tom.

"It sure does, but one could easily blow their diet, but that tidbit won't be mentioned," Babbs said.

"We outta flip flop the morning to afternoon," Tom amusingly added.

Both of their stomachs bulged in unison.

"Can you explain what Bernard was doing in the office?" Tom questioned.

"Something about working on his image," Betty replied. "Steve and Gary have put their heads together in Mr. Mosley's absence," she added.

"Wonder what plans they've made for us?" Martin mumbled.

She never noticed Tom's independent nature before. "What's your assignment today Tom?"

"Quiet in the community, guess focus on the autumn issues should begin. Who knows?" His mood was lurking between adventuresome and perilous. But after the boa episode the town seemed to have lulled.

"We've must get back and get the Thursday news on the street," she said as her car puttered toward Albemarle, stalling near Phieffer College.

They both watched two tangerine kites flutter and dive. At the end of the strings, two college kids looked backed, pointed, waved their balls as Betty and Tom gawked. She smiled, and a hand flapped up in a small wave, as if she'd known them all her life.

Martin said, "Pull over." She cranked the car again and Tom opened the door, camera in hand, as he started snapping. "Well we'll kill two birds with one stone," he smiled. Betty smiled at the flying snapshots.

Babbs said, "Do you see all the toes and books? Look at the seeded parachutes, hundreds of them drifting like white umbrellas opening the corners of this beautiful county."

Tom felt her aura, a mix of Southern pride and self-confidence. He opened his mouth – to say what he didn't know – but found himself unable to speak. The excitement held his breath and he thought Bakes could take lessons from her. Tom pleaded with Babbs to play hooky. They continued to stroll the college sidewalk. The sunlight was perfect and the urge to snap pictures had Tom reaching for his camera again. He smiles behind the lens, "This is really good stuff. So good in fact we've both lot track of the morning."

"You risk your job like you snap that camera and those comments," she said. Betty continued her speech, "Wise women choose their perils carefully."

"No argument from me," said the brown-eyed, food-chunking man.

Both bobbed like the kites in the wind. In fifteen minutes time they had pressed the medal back to Stanly Gazette. Betty exhaled, felt like humming. Her eyebrows bunched up, pretty dimples between them, and she laughed, answering her own questions with questions. Back in the office a splash on her arms brought her back from dreamland. Bakes tilted the water cup he was balancing on his head. Laughter surrounded them. Afternoon would remain a photograph as one of Betty's favorite pictures of life. She could feel the sunlight reddish and warm, the day swarming with butterflies, kites and glittering motes of sparkle.

Even though the day dawned bright threatening clouds suddenly appeared in the buttermilk clouds, followed by thunder and lightning. An ominous storm loomed over the scene that spread faster than the California wildfires.

Steve somersaulted into the newsroom, both arms outstretched, pointing his index at Babbs and his middle finger at Gary. Betty thought he couldn't imagine how he looked. His voice became crisp. For such an experienced reporter, she found he had a conscience where innocent bystanders were concerned. Committed, fear, uncertainty poured out his mouth. The excitement was growing, she realized facing the unknown challenge, and suddenly her feet were vibrantly alive.

She hadn't expected this reaction. It was if every facet of her mind and body were preparing for war. And that's exactly what it might prove to be, she thought ruefully.

He continued, "A developing story. The dam in Norwood has broken loose. Water is spilling fast and there's a band of homeless camped on the edge of the waterfront. Someone is going to have to help them out, figure the volunteer firemen will band together from all the surrounding districts. We need stories, pictures, front page details, NOW!"

The crew loaded up and pulled onto a dirt road, which apparently led to a frequented swimming spot and doubled as a lover's lane. They listened to the radio through the faint hiss of static. Betty felt herself settling, her head clearing, felt muscles she hadn't known were knotted up beginning to loosen and relax. For the moment it didn't matter what was ahead of them or what they would have to do come morning. Police sirens came tearing up the dirt road after them, their sirens blasting. The flashing lights seemed to give the group a sigh of relief.

The road was several hundred feet from the dam. Most of the structures facing the path where they'd turned were sparsely scattered, wearing uniform aspects of age, squalor and dilapidation. Betty saw gnarled figures withdrawn and spying the onset of rescuers. She stopped with the door half open, unable to plunge out into the picture, pinned in place by despondent sounds.

The bellies of the clouds coming from the south were dark and threatening, a stormy sunset color. Wind lashed the pine tops and shoved cones that straggled down from low-hanging branches.

"We're here," Steve said.

The wind got into the truck, and empty candy wrappers scooted around the vehicle's floorboard, rattling softly. The breeze stirred Betty's hair, flipped it in the wrong direction.

Conversations were overheard, "...How high is the water going to rise?" said one volunteer firefighter in a husky, almost abusive tone. A heavy man had spoken, judging by the wheeze when he exhaled, and continued to speak, "Do we have to worry about finding bums clogging up the dam?" "Your concern for the welfare of the homeless is touching," said a second man, this one with a thin voice.

They stood amid the flooding rocks; their sloping front door steps in the tent-strewn frontage. A great fit of shivering overcame Betty, her teeth clattered. The reality of the situation hit her like a sledgehammer.

Rises in the road delivered views deep into the woods, the feeling of strange uneasiness increasing. The road dipped where unseen whippoorwills cried and mosquitoes arrived in abnormal profusion to dance in the raucous piping of water frogs. A gloomy dam wall's hole invaded their nostrils with mold and decay.

The staff could feel the haunt of people that had invaded their miserable domain. The eyeholes that stared back were the only discernable facial features. Betty, Gary and

Tom were the crew accompanying Steve. He was grumpy and anxious upon their arrival. Late afternoon assignments meant a possible all-nighter. Gary pulled in behind a billboard that stated, "No One Beyond This Point!" It was as if the sign didn't exist. Tents, cardboard boxes and small doghouse looking structures dotted the landscape. There were generators, small kerosene lamps, and clothes strung between pines, apparently washed in the muddy water.

Betty had never witnessed anything like this and asked, "Does everyone know about this community?" Her heart pounded, and it was a struggle to breath, and she continued moving toward the water.

Gary and Tom exchanged looks. They saw her breath depart from her lips, as if she was standing in a walk-in freezer. Gary explained, "It's been a sore topic for a while. But the problem is this campsite is half on the Anson County line and half on Stanly County side. Local council members keep waiting on the other side to intervene. The government has bought up the land for public parks, doesn't leave the people on it, and insists that it's more important that the land be used for recreation for the people from the hot lowlands than the homeless people who inhabit it." He slipped a sideways look toward Betty. She was absentmindedly clutching her right hand to her chest, staring blankly at the wide-open scene. She had, until just a few moments before, been hiding the hand against her side. "Oh," is all Betty could say. No wonder councilmen hesitated when asked to revisit the homeless issue. A canoe stood upright with two paddles. The men shifted gears and water readied the craft.

"But we don't have life jackets," Babbs stuttered.

"No time," the men stated. All four heaved their bodies in the catfish-filled water. Gary's voice, in a slightly higher octave, one that cracked sometimes and lacked the resonance of a surer tone piped, "Let's go, NOW."

Tom commented, "I've heard there's fish in here big as humans." Gary stared.

Betty said, "Ya'll paddle, I'll pray."

Gary smacked against another rock, dented the canoe. The sound of someone slamming the craft into the water boomeranged their ears. When Tom called out, his voice wavered with alarm. He pulled a big wood sliver out of the front of his shirt, feeling the sting of pain beneath. It was a black graveyard of rocks and timber. Steve winced his eyes, scratched his head, binoculars swinging, and cleared his throat. He spat pellets of words, sounded like a bb gun in the wailing water. Tom was dizzy. The boat tilted underneath him. When he tried to balance he fell overboard – clinging to the canoe like a chimp on a gorilla, choking back the muddy ripples. The world spun and he waited for the water to stop moving. Not that it ever would. He was churning in the rapid spill and he couldn't block out the sickening whirl of it. He spat, wiped at his mouth. His stomach muscles cramped, as it he'd just done a hundred abdominal crunches.

Betty screamed. Her hands sprang to action, pressing her hands to her mouth to stifle the cry. In the same instant, Gary came to Tom's rescue and began to bark orders about how to grab him.

"Babbs, what are you doing, are you paddling?" Steve yelled. She had one arm on the paddle the balance of her body trying to secure Tom back into the canoe. The world wheeled around her, a kaleidoscope of too-muddy water, broken trees, and Tom Martin's chalky, horrified face. He was so close that her nose was practically stuck into the dark swirl of his hair. He inhaled deeply to breathe in Betty's sweet, reassuring scent, and then flinched at the lost balance of the canoe. Betty knew she should be feeling something – some alarm or urgency – but was instead off balance and dull-witted. Her ears were plugged up, and she swallowed continuously to make them pop. She felt as if she were trying to walk across a waterbed while inebriated. The canoe bed seemed to flex and wobble beneath her, and the sky tilted dangerously. He basically used her body to climb back into the boat. She trembled and her face was wet against his neck. He flipped over on his knees; found he was still holding one of her think wrists. Her nest of blonde hair floated around her head, bangs in her eyes. She hooked an arm under his armpits and pulled him up. Her knees were weak springs, all loose bounce and no support. No sooner than he comes to his feet he started to fall forward. He put his hands out to stop his fall and caught himself on her paddle. He was conscious of a building migraine behind his eyeballs, a deep, slow booming pain that threatened to become one of his all-time great headaches.

"Yes, and praying for guidance!" She exclaimed. Feeling the vermilion sludge turning the canoe, she turned toward his judgmental eyes. She felt weathered. It was darkening fast. Bernard and the girls had wheeled into a path above them.

A news's helicopter was circling above, rescue vehicles all over the grounds. Babbs searched the waters for clinging bodies. Tom's camera choked his neck, but his fingers were clicking madly, the wind moving his straight hair. They were drifting toward more danger signs when they spotted a clump of homeless banded together, hanging by blackened nails and horrific water pressure. The floodlight brightly blinded staring eyes of the destitute. Each face had a hungry, lost look, carried damp silence until they spotted the news's crew.

"Life is so cold and dark," one of the flood survivors later relayed to the news team. "We're desolate, and our lives are finished. There's nothing left." So many of them looked numb. They were all thinking about what had just happened to them and how their minds had wandered to the thoughts of death. The weight of all these thoughts presses them to quiet moments together. Water briskly flows and dim light flaps around them.

Betty wondered how many people could fit into a seventeen-foot canoe. There had to be at least five men and one woman in the clump. Visibility was bad, the yellow pine paddles were outstretched, and one-by-one the drifters were pulled to the craft. Crossing the river water was going to be treacherous. Fully loaded the men took control of the paddles, pushing against the current. Bakes was bellowing, outstretching broken cane poles toward them. Gary told them to jump, grab the cane and prayed Bakes and the girls had enough strength to pull each one of them into land. Dogs were close behind them. All along the banks rescue efforts were being made. There had to be at least twenty homeless.

As the crew walked back through the swampy mess the homeless village was scattered, destroyed, a board, cardboard, broken limbs all floating in the wild water. Betty took a reeling step backward, her face confused. In the seconds that followed, she found it difficult to make sense of what she was actually seeing. Time skipped.

Betty's reporter nature scrambled words. "Who'd clean up this disaster, where were these people going to sleep, what about their belongings?"

The dirt road was below water, their vehicle sputtered and stopped, sputtered and stopped. Ahead volunteers had log chains hooked to rescue vehicles hooking vehicles out of the muddy ruts. Daylight was fast approaching. The displaced water had taken its revenge.

Rumors were of the governor's arrival. Betty had seen catastrophes firsthand and knew this situation certainly met the criteria. She imagined they would all be on national news in the morning. Babbs was conscious of her long strands of blond hair pasted to her sweaty cheeks, and her color was back – cheeks flushed a pasty splotch of red, while the rest of her skin was bone white. She put the back of her hand against her forehead. Her bro felt feverish and damp. She looked up at the rest of the team and her chin began to tremble, and then she looked away. She covered her eyes with one hand. "Oh, God," she said. As they left for Albemarle no one spoke, all eyes focused on the corn fields and dairy farms where sliding-jawed cows turned soft eyes. Even they had moved to higher fields. Mist drifted.

"Look at the four of us," Steve said. "Aren't we a picture?" he coughed and lowered one of his eyebrows, raising the other, making a face that spoke, "We'll all be interviewed. Take credit where it's offered. Mosley would be proud of all of you." The pins-in-needles feeling in the air was subsiding, but only slowly.

In Bernard's SUV all three girls shuddered in theatrical ways. Their eyes had gone unfocused, fixed on the stage that lay out before tem. Goldie felt overcome for a moment by a sensation of light-headedness and profound disorientation. It was like a head rush from standing up too quickly on an empty stomach. Cookie felt the rotting feeling of having her legs give way, and the terrible hopelessness that the homeless must have felt as they were swept away from the plunge of water.

Stela said, "No way could a Dutch boy have plugged that hole." Her face had been scrubbed clean by tears and had become so pale it looked like wax, had lost even more color, taking on an echelon of translucence. Her breath thinned and she bit down on her lower lip. The other girls fell against her, their faces pressed hard to her chest. Stella put her arms around them, and they clutched each other, grasping at straws of humanity and faith.

Cookie strung her words together and wanted to know where the homeless would go.

Goldie explained, "Susan Hayes with the Red Cross has been contacted, and their preacher offered the church for a home base. There's a kitchen, bath, and cots. The pantry is full, so plenty of food. Everyone is welcome to a meal and a hot shower."

Her explanation and self confident statements stopped Bakes in his tracks filled him with wonder. The Stanly Gazette was an exemplary example of teamwork.

Bernard said, "We need to thank the Lord. There's no reason to worry. Everyone is going to be all right." The girls looked as dazed as he felt, blinking in the darkness. Somewhere, someone began to cry. Soon enough it sounded like a sad church chorus.

The police had blocked off Fork Road, which led to the dam area. They waved gloved hands at the rescue team, welcoming them back to safety. The round circles of people began to fade, going cool and blue, shrinking in on them. Then they winked out, leaving nothing behind except faint afterimages imprinted in the backs of each news's person's retinas. The news crew spent the next three hours pulling a special edition together for Friday morning. Washed-out images floated in front of them for the next few hours before fading away.

Dragging herself to the bathroom, she immediately makes the mistake of looking in the mirror. "Ouch." This could be worse than today. Staring back at herself she could easily be the "before" picture of a facelift. Betty felt as if she'd lost her best friend or even worse a coworker. One moment she was standing, shampooing her hair, and the next she was sitting down hard on the cold tile, water pinging off of her chest and legs, pressing her forehead into her palms as the sum of the night's events dripped off her. What made her the sickest was hard to decide. Closing her eyes she longed crazily for the water to melt her, to let it stream down the tub floor and slither her on down the drain. She was so thin that her bones pressed into the springs of her mattress. Although, she was tired, she knew she wouldn't be able to sleep, not today, tonight, and probably not in many more nights. The plight of the homeless had been temporarily suspended, but the world of cruelty appeared as shards stabbing her heart. Who could begin to describe the campsite scene and how the fact she hadn't even realized this situation could exist and how well the issue was kept out of the news from the remaining population of Stanly County?

Her headache and nausea was real, as her body heat intensified. She shut her eyes. It had been possible to view happiness and peace in her own square of blue sky, and now the sadness of destruction and near death events peeked back at her. Betty shook her head; there was a catch in her throat and the sounds she emitted resembled wails of the dreaded sirens that had cried desperately and broken in pauses. The pain began to rise inside her. A moan was struggled to force its way up from her chest. She wanted to put her forehead against a solid door of quiet, pull a deep breath down into her lungs and hold it, and let it go slowly. She drew a deep breath trying to ease of the tenseness of her muscles. Her face was clammy with sweat. Now wasn't the time for nerves. Being here was her choice. So she felt isolated and uncertain. She had to suck up this situation and face it.

As Betty stepped through the office door, Leo was talking into the phone, "Thanks so much." Leo faced Betty, "What happened out there? Was someone mean to you? Tell me, I'll make them pay," he questioned.

She rolled her eyes to hide her true emotions. "Where were you? Why weren't you there to help?" she asked.

He handed Betty a bodega coffee from the brown bag he was carrying. Starbucks had yet to make inroads to Albemarle. The fluorescent lights above hummed in his ears like an angry beehive. It sounded like someone stepping on bubble wrap when he rolled his neck. Leo stood straight, his back shoved against the wall, her shoulder blades in the shape of angel's wings. She usually swooned when she saw him, but this morning his charm couldn't turn her irritation. She felt a sudden ache in the pit of her stomach, a sensation of cold, sick weight. In the same moment, her head seemed to clear, shake off the cobwebs of exhaustion.

For two solid minutes he spun his pencil through his fingers like a baton twirler, his old creaking wooden office chair cawing as he rocked back and forth. Leo turned and squinted through office glass at the merciful still buzz of the other workers talking on the telephone. He placed his hands flat on Babbs's desk as he leaned over into her, his fingernails practically scratching tomorrow's review. "Steve and Gary decided I needed training, a weather camp in Lancaster, S.C. It was a two-hour drive there and back. More than an all day event," he explained. Secretly, he'd thought it was a diversion to keep him from seeing so much of Betty.

The girls had been eavesdropping for quite some time, hunched over until Goldie's long legs riddled with cramps.

Betty's universe had tilted, spun out of control in front of them. All of their hopes for a blooming office romance were washed away with the night before.

In the face of this disaster Stela propelled a suggestion. "Let's plan a benefit that can help the homeless and restore Betty's faith in humanity."

Three pairs of eyes and ears turned toward each other and tiptoed out of the hallway. The task wouldn't be easy but something fun and entertaining none-the-less. Their single thoughts had cross-stitched these individual's fate, binding a close-knit community even closer. Later that night they tackled others with their ideas. They would hold an old-fashioned cakewalk and games where a small fee would be charged.

Cookie was criticized for her outspoken thoughts, but secretly applauded for her daring challenges. Throughout the meeting Tom kept quiet; it was hard to relay or gauge what he had felt while he'd clung to the canoe for dear life. Afterward, he walked away without any words, and the others watched him suspiciously.

Mitch Mosley was in Todd's room when the developing story flashed Charlotte's local channel. They listened intently; as each of the news's crew were pictured and brief statements made.

The church on Anson Avenue flashed the screen as well and inside, as usual, the congregation was rocking the foundation.

He said to Todd, "Who'd ever thought they'd all suffered disaster?"

Even the ex-Lieutenant Governor and his wife had pulled up in their blue station wagon. He'd stopped at the Wal-Mart store in Wadesboro, and bought every possible item that could be crammed in the vehicle for the victims.

Mitch thought no wonder he was so popular. He looked at Todd and said, "How'd you like some Krispie Kreme donuts?"

Todd patted his waistline and replied, "None for me, watching the middle."

Mitch knew then things were changing, and for the better. His chest swelled with pride and for a moment he didn't feel so old.

He laughed, "Good for you. A break at last in your demeanor. I was getting tired of you being so tactless with me. You're a strange man.

"Strange is better than ordinary. Since my accident I swore I'd never be run-of-the mill again, and definitely not a cardboard figure stuffing my mouth instead of my brain."

15 - THE HOSPITAL VISIT

Sunlight angled brightly through the skylight, even though winds that day chilled the air. A stray beam of sunlight found its way through a piece of ruby-stained glass in the window box. It bathed the peer in a mist of shimmering colored light, and warmed her feet, neck and pale blonde hair. Birds soared in V-lines, driving the wind in perfect motion, past buttermilk clouds. Betty wished human interactions could be that smooth.

She'd gotten up earlier than usual, made biscuits, fried bacon and scrambled eggs. She wrapped four biscuits in foil, planned on leaving them with her boss. He had to be tired of eating hospital food. She phoned the office, reported her plans to drive to Charlotte.

Charlotte wasn't but an hour away and with movement on Highway 27 she made good time to the hospital. It had been two months since Todd's accident and she felt guilty not visiting more. But with Mr. Mosley's wife there now and Todd the serene afternoon coaxed her car into the paid parking lot, rolling to a slow stop in a back lot. The walk would be great exercise for her. She crossed the metal glass walkway between the main building and the parking lot.

Todd would soon be moving to the rehabilitation part of the hospital across the street soon. It was a slow recovery process.

Betty entered his room before visiting Mr. Mosley. Three nurses waved hello. Todd was glued to the cable and didn't realize he had a visitor. His peripheral vision had been damaged in the wreck. His manner was nice and very receptive. Laughingly, he said, "Babbs's cooking in the kitchen?"

With folded arms a doctor entered the room. She excused herself and walked to the end of the corridor. There sat a rocker and she gave it a jump-start with her foot. Questions of how many times Todd had stumbled the hallway surfaced. Being torn between strokes of her curiosity she walked back to his room. This time the television was off, curtains opened to a view of a floral garden below, and a huge smile expanded his face. As she glanced into the depth of his soul, his eyes danced. The word that came to her mind was lithe. Todd's attitude was lithe, powerful and a little docile. Gone were the timidity, irresponsibility, uncertainty, and sniveling niceness, and excruciating lack of self-consciousness that had encircled him since she'd know him for such a short time. A long hard look revealed a much trimmer Todd, almost handsome, and a newfound confidence. Babbs told him the kitchens were still waiting on him. He smiled and expressed he didn't think he was ready for them. Charm and wit sloshed out of his demeanor. His hospital garb sported dancing chili peppers. After noticing her exaggerated looks he explained how the nursing staff had the garb special ordered for him. In fact, he'd met an impressionable young woman named Ronnie. Amazing things, endorphins.

Her visit was fascinating and dinner hours fast approached. When the diet tray was delivered she excused herself, mentioned she was going to visit the boss. That his wife had been brought there, but Todd was already aware of the incident. No elaboration was needed. Betty left Todd and headed toward the part of the hospital that nursed Mrs. Mosley.

Glass doors, black granite floors, a high concave travertine advertised the names of wealthy benefactors.

Glassy depot for an unguided tour of ambiguity. A group of successful surgeons – goodness they're young – slouched by on paper-soled scrub slippers, humbled by long hours.

Babbs's own shoes were leather-bottomed and click-clacked on the granite. Ice-slick floors.

Crushes of humanity lined the lobby. A single phone sat in the middle of the trauma waiting room. People pulled chairs together, made makeshift beds. The smell was antiseptic, rubbing alcohol, sticky-ripe people that hadn't showered in days.

Betty eased her way through the waiting, looked for Mitch Mosley. No sight of him, she left the lobby, headed for the elevators. He emerged just as she arrived a cup of Joe in his hand.

"Let's go to the chapel?" Mitch suggested. He looked as if it were like pulling teeth to say that. She waited a moment and followed his lead. Half expecting to see a gathering, they rounded the corridor to emptiness and silence. The sound of comfort echoed this hall. No wonder Mr. Mosley wanted to slip away.

A beautiful spray of flowers sat near the podium and the prayer pews. When entering the room she looked straight into his soul. He was a good-looking older man, hair now noticeably streaked with gray. Looking back into her face her strong bone structure seemed stronger, more sculpted. Time had ignored her as she entered the front side of thirty. No wrinkles or laugh lines danced around her eyes. They hugged briefly.

"Can I give you my coffee?" her boss asked.

"No thank you, but I'll be glad to sit and listen, if you want to talk," Betty answered, pressing the four breakfast biscuits into his palms.

"You shouldn't have Babbs. But I do appreciate the gesture; food around here isn't worth writing about."

On that note she smiled and let her back rest against the grainy oak. She noticed how angled light filtered through the stained glass room, which was approximately fourteen by sixteen. Mosley had dwindled somehow in the last few minutes, shrinking into himself. Tones of light spilled in from two directions. A truckload of caffeine was exactly what Babbs needed right now.

Betty thought his voice was weak, and he didn't sound entirely sure of himself. She frowned, her brow wrinkled in contemplation, watching her moss. He seemed to be wary of her, calm and silent and drawn into himself. A brief look of pain and something like an apology flickered in her eyes.

At that moment he came undone. A choking sob escaped him letting loose everything behind it. Then Mitch doubled over into his lap with his hands clutched tightly over his eyes.

"I'm sorry," he said in a moan. His eyebrows were knitted together just the way her stomach felt.

"Peggy's still in trauma intensive care, her bed positioned next to the main station. Do you realize they put the worst cases next to the station? There's a single sheet draped over her body, no clothes beneath, still unconscious or either doped to the gill."

Betty exhaled, head positioned to listen. Mitch seemed so helpless. "Have you been eating, how about the children?" streamed from her mouth. Her reporter's nature surfaced.

"She's been through some real hell. Her brain has some swelling; they're talking about calling in a specialist to drill a hole in her skull cap." Some tears followed, but basically her boss was composed. He swiped his eyes and nose. "One of the best surgeons has been called in to consult. A metal-like cage will be placed around the bone structure to stabilize the fractures. Looks worse than it is, at least that's what you're led to believe. Let's focus on the positive. The news could be worse, at least the staff has her stabilized for now," Mitch added.

Betty teetered on the edge of an uncomfortable thought.

She thought for a moment, spoke softly, "Any neurological problems?"

"None mentioned at this point," Mitch responded. The cold in the chapel sapped him, so that he felt tired, felt his age. He couldn't imagine anything more foolish or weak than an old man pitching his despondency to another adult. Betty's boss felt disconnected for the first time in his life. His career, his friends, and the hard driving perseverance that had preoccupied him for more than thirty years seemed a matter of no importance now. Mosley felt he was a passive spectator to the actions of a God that surely had a message and purpose for him and his family.

She reached over and touched his arm. His eyes narrowed, his response was grainy with emotion. The quiet that surrounded them was a dreadful noise, amplified a hundred times. Betty could see he was so far into his thoughts that it was several moments before he moved. Mitch was thinking how he'd spent a lifetime trying to put distance between himself and the old man he now was.

"All we can depend on is the information from the staff and the good Lord above. The staff meets in groups and each one has to agree with treatment procedures."

Betty shuddered, "Let's pray together and head back to the trauma waiting room." Her steadfastness was a quality he was beginning to prize in her above all her other qualities. The way she took command stirred him, drew him out of himself. His shoulders twitched in reflexive surprise. He turned and looked. She was naturally pale to begin with, but now her face was bloodless, like polished bone. He wondered if it was a trick of makeup. "That's a good idea," Mitch said. "Family can only visit ten minutes every hour

or two, depending on the stats and if they appear stable."
"I hope your wife continues to improve," Betty told Mr.
Mosley quietly. She turned away from the pain in Mitch's
bloodshot eyes.

A drape of morning sunshine fell across their joined
hands as they bowed their heads. The light made him look
like a war veteran, his pants wrinkled, and shirt midway
down his thighs. Below this splash of sunshine were his
brown loafers, with his black-soled feet stuck in them.
Betty had never asked Mr. Mosley about his faith.

Mr. Mosley turned her and guided her into the hallway.
They walked toward the lobby and Mitch profusely thanked
her for visiting him, wished her well, adding to be very
careful in the evening traffic home, never asking about
the paper. She drove the hour's stint with a fat bundle
of pressing thoughts. Her car turned into the Wal-Mart
where she planned to buy food, but her feet carried her to
the fish and aquarium section, where two goldfish thrashed
at the surface's edge. She picked out a large bowl, fish
food, seaweed, and had the clerk net the gliding fish. The
bagged fish made her think of the carnival booth with
the ring tossing competitions. With her arms loaded she
headed to her car and finally home.

At the office in the morning meeting she was assigned
to revisit The Tiendos Mexican Restaurant, where she was
first ate with Todd. Lively festival music blared as she
entered and one arrow pointed to the food section and one
arrow pointed to the bill paying section. She remembered
the owner that was middle-aged and Hispanic, with old
eyes and a Cantinflas mustache. His stare and worker's
eyes were hypnotic. An older woman brought the menu,

asked, "Aren't you the senorita from the paper?" Her dialect was barely audible. Betty nodded a smiling yes. The older woman recommended starting with Caudillo for an appetizer and following with a plate of Beef Chalupas. She explained the name chalupas actually translated as "small canoes".

The fried shell was made from the same dough as tortillas, filled with meat, beans, cheese and shredded lettuce and tomatoes. Babbs had never experienced such a delicious lunch. The older woman also explained the green chilies were fresh-from-the-field. The cook brought her an added side dish of Fiesta Banana Cake for desert. He had used real butter and the sugar was sweet. On top were cherries arranged as flower petals for the icing.

Despite Todd's reaction, Betty now had a favorite restaurant. She lazily drove the back roads to the office and wondered if Leo liked Mexican food. Number one question to find out.

After leaving work Leo decided to stop by Betty's home. He rang the doorbell at 7:15 p.m. The neighbor's dog didn't bark, but his ears stiffened and his eyes followed him. Betty squinted through the peephole. Leo's face was a wide-angled blur, big grin, and he bared his teeth in a Halloween grimace. She laughed, opened up the door and they clumsily hugged. She hadn't had an opportunity to actually talk to him in several days.

"Well, looks like you have some new pets," as he glanced at the goldfish staring back at him. He picked at his tie and removed it. Babbs asked if he liked Mexican food. Assuring her he did, but had just finished dinner, they continued on to the den. She trailed him knowing the next time they ate out he'd be in for a treat.

"Admit that you write poetry in your spare time," Leo said. "You know everybody that's a reporter writes poetry, and doesn't dare admit it because they're self critical of their own work."

"Leo, what do you do, sit around all day and think of conversations to have with me when you drop in so unexpected?" she laughed. She glowered at him. "It's just that I don't want to hook up with any one particular guy at this point."

He reminded her of the lone sheriff in town, that strutted around with a pair of pistols on his hips. She's thinking he thinks of her as on old spinster that doesn't go anywhere. Little did he realize if she'd known of his impending call she'd opened that door like Marilyn Monroe with a made-up face, red lips, upturned lashes shading mischievous eyes, and would have just come from the salon sporting long painted nails. He'd have to swoon over her being elegant and wearing very high heels, and maybe she'd wrapped one of her grandmother's fox capes around her neck.

Betty blinked back to reality. She thought he was at least conscious of her existence, and the vanilla-cinnamon scents her new Glade freshener provided.

Time passed flowered and the change in her mood was truly remarkable. He spoke up, telling her morning would be there before they knew it and left. She turned and waved before she stepped back into her house and Leo always waved back, like a common fool, an idiot of a man who would have done anything to please her. Leo watched how her soft blonde hair floated around her head, held an eddy, airy look, and the shadows below her eyes drew his attention to how large they were. She smiled vaguely at him and he smiled back. After he left she wrote a quick letter home, did isometric exercises and watched the news. She thought there wouldn't be any trouble sleeping tonight.

Betty was awake in the dimness of the room for a long time later, listening to the muffled sound of the world beyond the drawn blinds and thought about her and Leo. Her thoughts lingered on how she soaked up close ups to identify people she knew.

When she finally managed to get to sleep, she had a wild nightmare about her father ferociously attacking her judgment in men. He was indifferent to her pleas, and she awoke agitated sweating, while it was still dark and the neighbor's dog was howling. Her baby blues glistened with mocking sparks at her interpretation of the dream. Her cheeks flushed, and she rocked back to sleep. During these minutes dreams reduced to piercing streaks of light and Leo transformed into a fuzzy mannequin rushing clumsily here and there.

16 - FALL FESTIVAL

In the month of November, when the oaks lost their leaves and the maples tuned gold all at once, the snakes slithering along Lake Tillery's shore searched for shelter. Hornets too, went looking for warmth having previously drilled holes in the ground, and passerby could hear their buzzing in rotten stumps. The pencil thin pines dropped their brown needles that laced the undergrowth of brush. The day had been the coolest in months, the first real day of fall. Morning was faultless; a redheaded woodpecker knocked on wood outside Babbs's home, tapping Morse code, waking her to smile. She knew something special was going to happen that day.

It was Saturday, a week after the flood. Her eyelids sank shut. She couldn't remember the last time she'd been so tired. Sleep kept pulling her steadily under, drowning reason, drowning sense, but as she went down again that image of Leo's face swam before her. She struggled back toward wakefulness. Time leaped forward. Even though emotions had burned the candle right out of her, she knew the day would hold the ingredients to mix up happiness once more. Leo would be there to pick her up in an hour. He was a man she could depend on, a steady jobber, and possibly could offer her a future she desired. She didn't know why she was feeling like a coon being treed. Thankful for the time, she made coffee and chose jeans and a pretty Alfred Dunner shirt to wear. Betty couldn't remember the last fall festival she'd attended. Her gaze leaped naturally to the window.

Betty and Leo looked across the lakefront up and down the roadside. Another gorgeous day. Blue skies rustled by piedmont winds and pencil thin pines. Town people scattered Indian Mound Road, back seats filled with coolers, visors, lotion, blankets, and children driving toward the limits of Norwood pulling into the park. The sunshine was intense and direct on their faces, a steady glare. They staggered in the heat, swayed backward, and brought their hands up simultaneously to shield their eyes from the light. Leo pulled out a pair of blind man's sunglasses, round black lenses with silver frames. They gleamed when they caught the sunlight. "Have you got a pair?" asked Leo. Betty nodded no. Leo's hands rested on the steering wheel. The black rubber immediately began to soften, melted to conform to the shape of his fingers. Betty watched, dazed, curious. The car was on the road, a long, curvy stretch of blacktop, punching through southern jungle, trees strangled in moss and mistletoe. The asphalt was twisted and unclear in the distance, through the flickering, climbing waves of heat. The radio's reception fizzed in and out, and Betty kept turning the knob, music overlapping a radio preacher.

In the park were Japanese trees flowered, the clean sidewalks that curved a perfect mile were lined with fragrance.

Gardenia, azaleas, and notes of color in the shrubs dotted a perfectly manicured lawn. The play equipment was like a block of climbing-in-and-out equipment straight off the lots of Mickey D's. Benches spread out for neighbors who wanted to gossip or just inhale the lavender. She could hear birds singing, feel the slowing pace of life and felt that if she became an old maid in this community it wouldn't be so bad.

The "Raise the Homeless From the Ruts" (not Betty's idea for a name of a festival) first annual fall festival was in full swing at the park. Across the street from Preacher Crane's church and junkyard swarms arrested the warmth. They looked like bees attracted to honey.

Leo wondered how this carnival had pulled into town and set up in such short notice. Tom Martin, camera in tow, was conversing with the town administrator and mayor. Two, people seldom seen together, chatting. Betty eavesdropped hearing, "Imagine, I'm cooking dinner, the lights blow out, and a low rumbling sound like an explosion echoes down the pasture road from me. I ran outside and heard screaming. "The dam has broken, the dam has broken!" My son-in-law calls me on the cell, telling me he can't get a hold of my daughter, Maggie." I yelled back at him, "Forget Maggie, I'll grab her and the kids and head in the opposite direction." In the background of our call I could hear the wall of watering roaring, images of the flow moving like a gigantic black snake, solid in enormous pressure. Then I thought out each tree it would take out one at a time, twisting in a path, maybe sparing one here and one there, plunging recklessly through the bridge across the adjacent side. Then I thought about those poor homeless souls I'd heard rumors of being in the midst of the nightmare. Although, I figured they were on the Montgomery County side, they would still be impacted. Yes sir, I'm glad our town could pull this grand event together today..." Betty smiled, remembered what the guys had told her about neither county wanting to be responsible. But, hopefully, after today it wouldn't be such a problem.

Geese on the pond rippled hypnotic suggestions. Leo had predicted a wonderful day and the temperatures were in the low 70's. She counted three different bands with concert benches posed in front of each of them. So many concession stands she couldn't tally straight. It seemed any type of food you could imagine was being served. Funnel cake, peach and apple cobblers, ice cream cones, slushies, hotdogs, and hamburgers, even egg rolls. Money flowed, fooled by the mood, a lullaby that promised beds for so many homeless folk.

Tom crossed the lawn and joined some more of the newsroom crowd. The girls, maintenance people, Bernard, Gary and Steve were all mingling. The air smelled like cocoa butter, fruit pies, and sticky sweat. Betty's thoughts drifted to the Piney Point Gold Club. Surely, there couldn't be many on the course today.

Tom was a snapping turtle, coming out of his shell, capturing treasured moments. Sunday's paper would be full of the shots. Betty had to laugh at Gary and Steve. When they got excited they ate. She was sure they were competing to see who could visit the most food vendors.

Each of the girls had teamed up with one of the staff to direct the games. At 10:15 a.m. was the first cakewalk. Ladies from the Agricultural Extension Club had outdone themselves. There were at least two hundred cakes to win.

And a tasting booth had free samples of Creamy Chocolate cake, Mocha Cheesecake, Spiced Black Walnut cake, Lemon Coconut cake, Decadent Fudge cake, Banana-Nut Layer cake, Raspberry-Fudge cake, Strawberry cake, Ambrosia Cake, Caramel cake, Hummingbird cake, all types of pound cakes, and finally a Better-Than-Sex cake.

You can only guess which line was longer for the free samples. A precise square of chalked lines approximately forty feet by forty feet divided into twenty two foot spaces with the numbers in the middle were colored by chalk. A round cage with numbered balls was located in the center of the cakewalk. Stela pulled the numbers and Tom delivered the cakes to the winners. Each person paid five bucks for their block and five blocks won each time the game was played. That was seventy-eight slots times five dollars each hour. There were five games timed out in an hour's time, with fifteen minutes in between. Just think three hundred and eighty five possible dollars times five. If all the slots were filled it would be one thousand nine hundred and twenty five dollars donated to the fund. Betty quickly calculated the money.

Behind the park was Mabry's Dairy Farm and several of the older people had gathered fifty cows that would be let out to roam the roped off pasture.

Cow patty bingo. The squares were numbered with lines and chalk. Whichever cow decided to take a dump (preferably called a cow patty) and landed in the participant's square would win twenty-five dollars. Only fifty people could play at a time and the game was limited to an hour and a half. If one of the cows did their duty before the time expired another game started. Five games were lined up along with the betters sporting binoculars.

Cookie and Bakes were the official spotters and money-deciding judges. That was possibly another two thousand five hundred dollars if all the spots were sold, even more if the cow chewed the green appetite driven.

A tourist bus transported people to Colson's Creek where a Civil War reenactment could be witnessed. Authentic costumes were worn and each school bus could haul fifty people to the site. And at three dollars a pop every two hours the money added up. There were three enactments scheduled.

Golf carts carried tourists for free rides through the historic district and donations were gladly accepted.

Cookie and Steve were manning the panty hose race. Legs of stockings had been cut at the straddle so one leg would hang from the participant's belt loop. Before attaching the loop an orange was inserted. The player had to swing their pelvic section forward to move the orange in the stocking against the orange on the ground ahead. The first one to cross the finish line won five bucks. Ten players paid two dollars a piece to try and win. Betty and Leo's job was to award the winner and collect the starting fees.

Babbs loved it all. She hung on Leo's arm and he herded her into the excitement. All the small town grace and good taste were embedded in his DNA. Betty adored him, just like everyone else. Out of her peripheral vision she saw a cluster of homeless, redressed in newly donated clothes and shoes, enjoying the entertainment. They stood amid the noise and excitement inhaling with their lungs, exhaling away all their troubles. Betty knew this moment would linger in her thoughts for a lifetime. Life was so strange. Leo even felt comfortable enough to play with his inner gorillas. Something about this last thought gave her a nervous jolt, as if she'd slid on shag carpet and touched metal, catching a sudden stinging zap of static electricity. But she was caught up in the moment and her new life and new job, as a food critic seemed to be the height of her being.

Babbs was enjoying explaining the history of ice cream to Leo, how high up in the Quingling Mountains, a little boy named Li Po figured out how to flavor snow and the rest was history ending with two guys in Vermont. What she was building up to was asking him if he'd like to go to a new Hawaiian shaven ice eatery that had opened above Albemarle and of course she was licking the Peach ice cream as fast as she was talking when Cooley summoned them.

"There you are! Come! We've gotten some great news. The mayor is at center stage accepting a huge donation, actually two," Steve exclaimed.

The mayor tapped on the microphone and the crowd lulled to a squeaky silence. "One of our local town members has generously donated a five thousand plus square foot three story house down toward the railroad tracks. It's close to the stores and businesses and we can renovate the huge domain into a shelter for the homeless and other persons suffering mishaps. The governor is setting up grants our town can apply for to maintain a small staff and the Stanly Community College and the Employment Security Commission has joined forces to host training and a Job Fair in the next few months. And the grand finale is the one hundred thousand dollars Alcoa Foundation has presented. The money raised from the fabulous turnout is icing on the cake. Just a play on words people. Maybe I should say cakewalks."

Musical sounds hummed through the crowd and all

hands extended in midair. Everyone was whirling with excitement, even Bakes was shifting one foot to another.

"Now, I'd like to invite the main people who pulled this event tighter to join me on stage." One by one each of the staff was called forward along with numerous other individuals. Twelve pastors were in the group. Betty remembered Steve's advice.

The tally of money at the end of the day was over two hundred thousand dollars and a structure to house the unfortunate. The sky, pond, and even the geese looked radiantly alive. Betty didn't gurgle a single sound, but joyous tears spilled over her eyelids in a flood, washing her face and neck. Her heart soared. Leo felt like crying. She pressed her forehead to his breast. Her breath rose toward his face, and for a moment they both swayed, as if they were dancing very slowly. When their composure returned he looked at her face again. "Let's pray, Leo, together." It was conceivable that they were perfectly matched. He reached in his pocket and handed her his handkerchief.

Betty loved imaginary places and felt Norwood was similar to the Island of Blessed, which was home to people that dressed in beautiful purple spider webs. In spite of being bodiless they moved and talked as mortal beings. Naked spirits. The capital of Blessed was built with gold and lined with walls of emeralds. Around Blessed ran a river of exquisite perfume, easily navigated, several rivers of milk, and fountains sprouting pure water, honey and perfume. The community constantly bathed in twilight, as if the sun had not yet risen and it always was springtime. Norwood's similarities brought about these peaceful visions and she felt truly blessed.

17 - PROGRESS

Monday's morning meeting was positive. The entire office felt like a newly decorated scene, chat was upbeat, staff was exchanging smiles, and plans for the workday flew around the room. Betty's assignment was lunch at a new Italian restaurant. It had opened near Troy off of 24/27 Highway, still on the Stanly County side. Its name being Caccagna surprised Babbs, as the study of imaginary places was her hobby. She recognized the business name as a small country not far from Germany. According to people that traveled there you could only enter the country through a river. The new restaurant was built on an island in-between the Pee Dee River. You were rowed to the shore or had the choice of a speedboat to cross.

In the middle of Caccagna (imaginary) a volcano filled with boiling broth sprouted. From its bowels ravioli and pasta stirred. Slopes were cheese covered, falling into a vale of melted butter. Soil produced truffles as large as houses, the rivers full of wine and milk. In winter the mountains were covered in cream cheese. All the houses were made of Italian food and the bridges were big salami.

It was rumored people that wanted to reduce their age only had to wash in the fountains. Women gave birth singing and babies immediately walked and talked after being born. There was much more to the 16th or 17th century story, but her memory failed her.

Upon entering the new restaurant the hostess was pregnant and much of the serving staff. Betty wondered if it was a requirement. A volcano mural depicted the scene of her imaginary world and a volcano-shaped fountain was in the center wall dividing sections. Such an odd sight for a small community.

Italian food smells assaulted her senses. The menu special, "A Pasta Supper", for $8.95 enticed her. It consisted of fried mushrooms, Beefy Tomato Stuffed Shells, Mixed Green Salad with house dressing, Garlic Bread with Herb Butter, a huge Tiramisu House desert, wine and coffee. The owner, Antonio Picklesimer Pieroni approached her, chef's hat stilted, turned up eyes, dimple chin, dark wavy hair. His nameplate spread across his chest and beneath his name a small Chef/Bottle-Washer/Owner plaque. He had a sense of humor. Babbs had to smile. Red checked table clothes, fresh flowers and heavenly food choices. He was bound to succeed. His name gave her thought to ponder, a German middle name with Italian first and last name. Antonio must know about the imaginary country with his mix of German and Italian blood searing his heart.

"Call me Tony," he said.

"Call me Betty Babbs."

He snickered at her name seeing the size of her breasts, immediately associated Babbs with boobs, and curiosity

146

broke loose from her jaw. "Your name, the restaurant's name, an Italian comedy?" she asked.

His pregnant wife floated their way. She was a *so-attractive-I'd sell-my-soul-to-the-Devil* type. "I'd wager anything he'd go to bed with you to get a five star rave. He grasped her hand and kissed it.

"Are you forgetting I'm very married?"

Betty laughed at the comedy and was pleased with the formality to which the couple had resigned themselves. She knew the some restaurateurs would sacrifice anything for the sake of their business. But, Antonio's wife was the faithful loving wife, and he the faithful loving husband. She knew it wasn't a fairy tale.

He smiled. "Just enjoy, and I'll read your review." So he knew who she was. She really expected a five star review and that was what he received.

Betty left feeling that her dinner was the best experience of her life there. Tony explained the meaning of the dessert to her. Tiramisu in Italian means "carry me up" or "pick me up." She found this dish so ethereal, she felt as if she had been scooped up to Heaven. Babbs decided she would have to diet a week for eating all of the luscious layers of whipped cream mixed with buttery mascarpone cheese and ladyfingers flavored with coffee. And that was saying a lot because she absolutely adored Tiendos. "Who'd know two favorite places to eat!" she exclaimed to herself. The trick was going to get Leo to try either place.

After lunch, Betty headed back to the office, walking into the bullpen wearing a pinky-pink pashmina scarf wrapped around her hair and blue cat shaped sunglasses. She always wondered what she'd find upon her return. On the ride back she circled the tip of a channel, noticed a unique section of lake front property that faced the restaurant. Every few miles she passed a window box with flowers tumbling over its edges followed by a wrought-iron gate a few feet away. She peeked through the gates and behind the houses were magical gardens of clipped and shaped boxwood topiaries, azalea, rose beds, and hand-pruned bushes. There were plantings of monkey grass bordering the beds. Ivy climbed most of the chimneys and heavy decorative pots overflowed with brightly colored mums. The entire area was bewitching. Betty longed to trespass the afternoon away, peep through the windows to see how the richer half lived.

Upon return to the office the girls were in a deep-seated conversation of how they could help Mitch. He'd practically taken up residency at the hospital. His wife was now in a private room and he never left. They weren't gossiping, but discussing how they might be able to make a difference, maybe spruce up his yard a little for him since it had been neglected for over two months. They all decided to talk to the guys and take Saturday to meet at Mitch's house early in the morning.

Surprisingly, Mitch Mosley resided in the development, an assortment of Ranches and Tudors with brick, stucco, and vinyl with various sherbet shades – peach, lemon, lime – laid out along streets that were named lanes and twisted in loops. They drove by it twice before the guys spotted the number on the mailbox. His home was colored a mango shade, reminded her of a caution light, and wasn't in any particular architectural style. Just a big, bland American suburban. Betty wanted to escape and peep into the windows. His family's house was in the middle of a circle, deep in the sub-division. They pushed open the heavy gate and everyone gasped. The flowers in his planters were dried, crisper than dried fruit in a dehydrator. The yard area hadn't been mowed in months. The roses were spindly and each leave was heavily black spotted. Forgotten shovels, rakes and garden tools had been dropped and left, and the outdoor patio table glass was crusty with algae. The angel fountain sputtered and the irises were in desperate need of cutting back, as well as the pampas grass.

"Oh Lord," everyone said in unison. "Do we have a plan?" one of the girls asked. They all held their breath.

"The fountain's fish are dead and full of green gook," Goldie said. She climbed the edge and gazed down. The water lilies had become thick clumps of strangling overgrowth. Even the deck had greened and was in desperate need of Clorox spray.

"These are all fixable things," Gary offered. "Now guys and girls someone could probably puncture a tire with our attitude." Steve stood with his hands on his hips, and Bernard just shook his head. "I had no idea," Tom expressed with concern.

They needed to get into the garage area and see what type of supplies Mitch had to help with the much-needed manual labor.

"Check the door to the garage," Leo said. "He probably didn't even lock the house. Just walked out and drove straight to the hospital."

Tom opened the door to Mitch's home, poked his head in. The lights were off, and with the sun on the west side the room drowned in blue shadows. Sure enough, Mitch had left the door unlocked, and the guys walked into the garage, as any robber could. The ADT wasn't even set. On their right side was the mowing and trimming equipment. On the left side were a wheelbarrow, potting soil, thirty-gallon trash bags, and a sprayer that could be utilized to clean the deck.

The girls went one step further and entered the house. It was not in as bad in disarray as the yard, but the entire house could stand a thorough cleaning. Mainly, mopping, waxing, vacuuming, Windex and pane action, plus dusting. This was manageable. They would work inside and let the guys work outside.

Everyone was trying to figure out what to do first when Betty approached the guys outside. They informed her they were going for gas for the lawn mower and trimmer. She instructed them to buy some small potted mums she could replant in the window boxes, and that the girls would be inside working.

Inside they filled the dishwasher, folded clothes in the dryer, and made the master bedroom, finally cleaning the bathrooms. Next they Windexed, dusted, and then vacuumed. Stela gladly commandeered the machines. Betty tackled the bed and Cookie did the bathroom. Goldie dusted. In the end they all worked together.

Betty found the record player and the old 45's. They danced to Elvis, listened to the Buckinghams, and danced the Watusi. They all sang backup to the Motown songs they knew. "123 Red light" was one Betty had almost forgotten. The guys heard the sounds as they drove up. Each stared at the other and rushed inside to see what was going on. One would have thought they'd discovered Lucy and Ethel up to old tricks. Laughter was boisterous. The girls looked into the fridge to see what they could dish up for snacks, knowing the guys would be ravished after all the yard work.

In fifteen minutes time they had all loaded into Gary's truck and headed to the local grocery. They drove back and walked up the steps with a bag of groceries each, dumping them onto the floor in the hallway.

"There's more in the truck," Goldie pitched toward Steve. "Come help me before I drop dead, even though I'm already drop dead gorgeous."

Betty walked outside, watched the flirting between Goldie and Steve, then carefully picked up the potted mums and started work on the window boxes. Babbs thought about Goldie's fondness for romantic novels that fueled her fantasy as a heroine being swept away by Prince Charming. Steve could be that guy. Betty watched how Goldie's head raised, and her gaze was fixed on Steve. Her eyes flashed a bright wink. He was staring directly back at her.

Vigorously, the work started and she even cleaned the panes on the outside in front of the house. Too much house to tackle in one day. Two hours later they were all slumped on the clean patio eating off the scrubbed glass.

"Hope Mitch approves of this, I might need an organ some day, that is if he's an organ donor," laughed Bernard. "He might string us all up by something for doing his place," said Cookie. One might know she'd sex the moment up.

"Tell you what," commented Goldie. "I'm going to miss work tomorrow."

Betty stared, said calmly, "Goldie, tomorrow is Sunday, you know church day?"

Laughing Goldie said, "I knew that, wondered if any of you tired humans would catch on." They all burst out in laughter.

Gary unloaded all of them at the office where they'd met and parked their vehicles.

Leo said good-bye to Betty, and he promised to call her later, then Tom lazily walked to the three remaining girls and said, "God, I almost feel like I just got married!" Steve and Bernard drove off, listening to the chatter.

As soon as Betty entered her house, the phone rang, and it was Leo. She envisioned Sparks smiling through the phone. He informed her that he's coming over for a little while.

"What we did was good!" he exclaimed. She agreed. Finally, the timing was right and she asked him if he'd like to go out and eat after church tomorrow. They hung up, agreeing to attend The Church of the Nazarene and then Betty could drag him anywhere she wanted. She knew it would be to the land of imaginary Caccagna.

Gary Leatherwood walked barefoot between the white crushed stone and pine needles that had recently surfaced in his backyard. A timid wind had rattled Mimosa leaves as he neared his backyard. He could see the empty beer bottles that overflowed from a garbage can on his neighbor's pier.

He thought about the headaches they must have suffered this morning while he was working.

At the corner of the wet side of his lot he could see Betty's backyard. The crass crunched beneath his feet. Her house was dark. And the only sound he heard was the cricket's furlong song. He was nearly to the steps when lantern lights from her yard started flashing. He thought what the heck. Confused, Gary decided to go for the binoculars. Not that he was a peeping Tom. Even with them it was too dark to tell who might be in the backyard. A male was chasing Babbs in a playful fashion. Gary knew or at least suspected he knew who was chasing her. It had to be Leo Sparks. Lately, Leo's extra time had been spent cruising their neighborhood.

He fought back a bad case of snorts and felt like a spy, but this was too good. He backed against a tree, his silhouette blending with the shadows, wished he had Tom's camera so he could snap the scene and send to the office, announcing that in his view of the iniquitous exploitative nature he'd been made a victim of an undeniable romantic spectacle. Leo had caught Betty, first a quick peck, then a second, and finally a crushing kiss. Her gaze was questioning, as a pretty furrow wrinkled between her eyebrows. She shot him a snorting, contentedly happy look – the one of a child that had purposely-splashing mud on a fresh washed vehicle. The scene jumped her, and halted her in her tracks.

Quietly, he tiptoed up the walkway and entered his own home. His back door closed without a squeak. Pulling the binoculars for one last long look out the garden window he spied on the couple slow dancing. He saw the slam of a body against a tree. Leo and Betty were lip locked in a kiss so deep it was difficult to see either of their faces. His hands were sliding down her back, and his shirt was already off, tossed onto the unruly heap of leaves next to them. They were moving perfectly in sync, without stopping.

Watching them he felt like an intruder. His heart lurched, all the blood rushing to it in a sudden, adrenaline burst. He should have asked her out more on Sundays. But she wasn't sporting an engagement ring yet. Gary decided to intervene and see if he couldn't win her heart. He grabbed a six-pack of Pepsi and dropped in on Betty and Leo. That should break up the lovey-dovey mood for the evening and besides he was bored. Gary toting the six-pack grabbed his keys and his sandals, and headed a block over. He drove. His palms were sweaty and slick on the wheel, his stomach agitated. When he watched them he almost wanted to slam his fist into something. He was driving too fast.

The buzzer was going crazy. "Come on in Gary, a surprise. Leo is here and we're just talking," Babbs said after inviting him in. Gary thought other thoughts.

"I didn't realize you had company," he responded. Betty smoothed over her tilted hair and rearranged her blouse. Hopefully, a small fib that wouldn't head him Hell bound. Leo glares at Gary. "Well aren't you at least going to say hello to Leo?" Betty asks.

"Hello Leo," Gary parrots, his eyes not budging from Betty. Leo whacks his elbow on the chair and she does everything not to smile. In his effort to keep Gary in the dark about any relationships Leo has mastered the art of complete indifference toward her when the three of them are together. So much so it's comical. Not to mention, pretty smart.

"I don't know what I'm doing here like a third wheel with you two," Gary spoke. Leo thought what a joke, mumbled a low amused murmur. He didn't mean for him to hear him talking to himself, and maybe not even completely aware he'd spoken aloud. After all, their houses were only divided by water. He'd probably been spying. Leo lifted his shirt over his head slipping back to a more relaxed stance.

Plopping in the chaise lounge between Leo and Betty he felt Leo's glare. The drinks banged heavily against the table, and she flinched at the sound. Her eyebrows furrowed, and her mouth opened in a way that suggested she was about to say something. Her stare, however, remained fixed on some abstract point off in the water before her. Babbs peered at the full moon hiding behind clouds. She immediately asked Leo if it was supposed to rain. Sparks shook his head and answered a definitive no.

There they were three reporters, three friends, drinking three sodas on a serene Saturday night. A brief pause. In the silence they all reclined, looked skyward.

Leo shifted his gaze to Gary. "Well what's up Gary?" Leo asked.

Gary knew he was acting like an adolescent. But so what? He wanted her to pay attention to him. And why shouldn't he? He was a catch.

"I came over to ask Betty about going to church Sunday, and maybe a dinner date," he replied.

Both looked straight at Betty. "Oh," she said. What a predicament she thought. "I already have plans this Sunday, but next Sunday would be fine." She wanted to cover her eyes and keep two fingers apart to peek between them.

Sitting in between them with moonlight slowly closing in, Gary was enticed with her direction – the fullness of it – through her eyes and laughter; he discovered the attraction was even stronger than he thought.

She studied Leo, and then she studied Gary. She was lost. Caught and swept adrift by two men. It seemed the word canoe kept popping up where she was concerned. Now she felt like she was in a toilet paper canoe, sinking fast.

"That's great Babbs!" Gary said under the spray of Leo's cold stare.

Babbs noticed how Leo's eyes sparkled when he was mad, and his rigid complexion took on an appealing blush.

"We can eat at Tiendos if you want?"

Betty had wanted to revisit the restaurant, and eagerly accepted. Leo felt like the butt end of a bad joke.

He actually thought Betty was settling down for a relationship with him. It was then he released a sigh, stood up, explained tomorrow was church, and since he had plans he should head on home. All the while winking at Babbs.

Gary added, "Me too." He leaned toward her to deliver a kiss on the cheek, smelled her sweet breath – and Leo's aftershave.

Both exited and Betty lingered a little longer, staring out

of bed at the distant and cloudy night sky. Her backyard had stretched into a competition match.

It was Sunday and her eyes hung over the alarm, pressing the ten-minute snooze button. Didn't seem like a minute had passed before it alarmed again. Betty ordered herself out of bed. It took her a moment to realize what a grand day it would be. Still drowsy she opened her closet and began humming. Standing between the two lines of clothes she decided on a pastel green suit. It would be nice to wear to Caccagna later. Babbs started laughing, thinking back to how the evening had ended.

Leo glanced over his shoulder, admired the slice of daylight that beamed across town from Betty's house. He smiled and looked forward to seeing the highlights her hair would sparkle and bounce against. Sparks dressed quickly, throwing a green sports coat over the pastel green shirt. His and Betty's mind were in sync and neither had a clue.

As they entered The Church of the Nazarene Leo's mom and dad beamed at each other. Their only son was escorting Betty to their pew. She clung to his side, as they seated near his parents. His mother reached over, patted her hand, and smiled. "You'll never be alone in Norwood. We're your extended family now, Betty. All of us." She hadn't gotten up the nerve to accept a luncheon invitation from them yet. They might get the wrong impression and think the couple was getting serious. This thought jolted Babbs and she had to ask herself if they were. Shrugging her shoulders she dismissed the thought. The preacher asked all to bow their heads together in pray and the morning service began.

Gary arrived late, and plopped in a position next to Betty's right. Leo and his family were lined on her left. Pastor Bob, knowing his congregation's activities, thought these rowdy men wouldn't last a month of Sundays. Leo was thinking what a hair-brained scheme. Betty felt orphaned between the men; know that really all that existed were their lives as young professionals. Pastor Bob noticed that the pews were filling fuller, maybe due to the ongoing saga. But, he didn't care as attendance was up.

Leo's mother was a pale woman who had been handicapped for close to eight years and looked after her son with devotion. Leo had explained how his father had named him Leo, since his mother's name was Leona. Betty felt an odd sensation in the pit of her stomach. She really hoped his mother would get better as time wore. On. She just couldn't understand why this nice young lady hadn't accepted any of her invitation to lunch or dinner after services. His father was also very fond of Betty.

18 - CHALLENGES

Betty had arranged her hair carefully, put on a dab of perfume, lipstick and blush, manicured her delicate hands, and lengthened her already long lashes with mascara. She wore a delicate but simple black dress with matching pumps and her black pearls, South Sea pearls, large as marbles – roped around her neck. When Leo spotted her, his eyes lit up and his heart skipped several beats.

"Hey beautiful," he said smiling.

"Hey, yourself," she said, holding out her arms.

It was a very beautiful night for a lengthy ride to the new restaurant, Caccagna. Along the way she delved into the conversation about her love of imaginary places and the little knowledge she knew regarding this restaurant's name. She also informed Leo about the Chef/Chief Bottle Washer/Owner, Antonio. How he had two Italian names and implanted in the middle was a definite German one. Both laughed tender murmurs. Betty knew the restaurant would work for them. The Crepe Myrtles out back were in full bloom and the interesting local art on the walls were enough for conversation. Mingling between the delicious cooking smells and candlelight would make the perfect evening.

She'd called ahead and made a special dinner request, which was to be a surprise to Leo. The menu tonight would be a Bacon-Topped Cheese Ball, Garlic Bread with Herb Butter, Spicy Manicotti, Orange and Pear Salad, Spicy Gazpacho, Tomato-Topped Asparagus and Mushroom-Stuffed Beef Tenderloin for the main course. Desert was Decadent Fudge Cake or Peppermint Ice Cream Pie. For all she cared he could eat both.

Betty's head was spinning like a blender on ice crush. The very pregnant young waitress beamed with elation as she topped off their glasses, almost as if they'd just granted her a once-in-a-lifetime-wish. Behind her, the pale stonewalls of Caccagna glowed like a Tuscan sunset. Leo was thinking if it could have gotten any more disgustedly perfect. His heart floated like the bubbles in his glass. "Well, what do you think?" she asked. "The pasta?" He said, "Bellissimo." Betty was still spinning when their waitress came back fifteen minutes later. "Some cappuccino signora?" "Si," Betty said, leaning back on her banquette, basking in the golden glow of night. Once more their rotund waitress asked, "Anything else?" pushing the four-figure calorie loaded dinner check across the table.

He picked up the check and pulled her close, cupping her hands in his, tracing her fingers with this thumbs. "Tonight is like heaven," he said tenderly. She blushed just a bit and her eyes opened wide.

The meal completed, they pushed back their chairs, summoned their waitress and settled their tab. Leo left an impressive gratuity. Each rose and walked out onto the pavement. He had his arm around her shoulder. She had her head against his neck.

"Perfect moment for love," she said, "almost as good as inducing it."

"Almost," he answered.

As they departed the walkway and approached the back of the restaurant they heard screams. They didn't know what else to call it but screams. The pitch started low, as if it had bubbled out of the volcano in the center of the building itself, and rose to rasping and livid levels. It should have burst the center of the building open, causing spirits to materialize from the dead.

"Let's not involve ourselves with this," Betty whispered, and by the light they saw a mounded group of pregnant women. She felt her throat closing. Antonio was spurting a foreign language – German, Italian, or a combined Italigermane? The woman was writhing in his arms. People were gathering immediately around him, stopped their conversations to gawk and listen. Betty at least made an effort to be discreet.

Leo for one wasn't going back inside. He turned and apologized to Betty and said, "I've got to help." His eyes darkened. Betty retreated and immediately started worrying about the woman.

Babbs glared at him. Maybe the girl is in trouble she said, "She looks drunk."

"Whatever it is, it is a situation," Leo spat back. "We live in a modern world, not an imaginary one." The voice that came out of him could have been a falling comet, crushing her on the scene. He called 911 and summoned help.

There was a brief pause. Betty replied, "I see." Leo bit his tongue. "Didn't mean to sound so harsh."

She had never experienced anyone in labor. It literally scared her to death. Leo assured her it was normal behavior. The woman was trying to whisper, but her voice choked, and when she forced her next breath up; it came out shrill and wavering. "Make it stop, Antonio." Everyone was watching, crosscurrents of worried murmuring rattled the customers; people didn't want to miss what might happen next. The other pregnant waitresses jumped out of the way.

"Anyway, who in their right mind would hire so many waitresses in their third trimesters?" Both turned to Antonio.

Betty wished she were a doctor. But she was not a doctor, just a reporter on a date, witnessing a painful event. She watched the others, then Leo, who had calmed the crowd and the shrieking woman. It turned out it was Antonio's wife. Her face was dazed and expressionless, her eyes troubled, the eyes of someone in a zombie state. In the yellow beam of sunlight that fell through the door, her skin was so pale and fine it was almost translucent, looked as if it would bruise at the slightest touch. Babbs squinted back at Antonio's wife, took her hand, and steadied her on her feet. The night would be long.

The woman started yelling again, "I'm going to kill you."

Everyone was frightened. He was glad for our company. The crowd heard engines revving behind the, furious growls of sirens sounded, rising to a roar, headlights splashing through the walls of water. The medics arrived in speedboats and transported them both to Troy Hospital, since it was closer than Stanly. Their eardrums hurting from the shrill began to clear and from a long way off, the wail dimmed.

Betty knew none of them would forget the conflagration of hysterical and feeble thrashing or pain Antonio's wife felt for some time. Questions about marriage and a family were the furthest thoughts from her mind. Antonio had been chain-smoking like Popeye the Sailor Man, and his hair slicked back, black like Brutus reminding her of Olive Oil.

Leo put the car into drive and began to roll them to Betty's home. She fell silent. The sound of Betty trying not to speak was somehow worse than if she'd repeated what had happened over and over. He was quiet too, but mostly because he was trying not to laugh. He saw how serious her face was. He had begged her to go someplace else after they left where there were lots of people and bright lights, so they could get past this night. "We can figure this out. Do you hear me?" He couldn't remember her logic for not going. Logic was out the window. He wondered about her hush-hush attitude — or, more explicitly, the poignant entanglements that might come with knowing them.

She didn't even invite him in. Leo thought this was not a good thing. He pulled her close, but she didn't respond, her body rigid, uncooperative. She still wouldn't look at him, wouldn't look anywhere except behind his head.

"See you tomorrow Leo."

"Okay, you going to be alright?"

"Yes, just tired."

Leo identified with her futile feelings. He loved her and winning her reciprocation was going to be hard work. But, he didn't want her to reject him and didn't want her to think of him just as a puppy panting for her attention. He touched her chin, lifted her face toward his, and studied her high cheekbones and her eyes that watched him back. He drew his hand away.

Betty suddenly felt like a guppy swimming among sharks. She'd arrived at the concept of her beliefs of God from what amounted to a genetic push. She was raised Southern Baptist, believed in the Trilogy, knew God was all-powerful and that if you didn't live by the Ten Commandments it would be a harsh price to pay. Her mother always told her to marry for love. Her father looked back and said love doesn't pay the bills.

She knew life and love was work. She'd witnessed it firsthand with Antonio and his pregnant wife.

When Babbs rested her thin frame, falling into thoughts of how literature was her passion, and how she'd never compared Leo to any of the characters she'd studied until tonight. She thought about what sort of old married couple they'd make. She imagined herself white headed and Leo with tufts of gray growing out of all the wrong places, his ears, nostrils. Big, wild hairs sticking out of his eyebrows.

Betty often compared her expectations of men to knights. Marie, Countess of Champagne was a famed and respected patron of the arts. Chretien de Troyes, the greatest poet of her time, and probably a member of her royal court wrote a poem named Lancelot about ladies and their knights. Marie had believed true love couldn't exist between married couples because it could not exit without jealousy. And it seemed there were always issues of jealousy and commitment in a relationship. So did she agree with Marie and think true love could only exist without jealousy? Leo was a knight, she was a lady. Most of the men on the news's staff fell into the characters of different knights. Knights were also destined for the church. She'd have to sleep on these thoughts.

There was a sentimental restructuring in the office, and everyone was in a daze. The staff fell in and out of love, and when they arrived at church they often weren't with the one the week before. But the important thing to remember was they did attend church services.

19 – GOOD NEWS

There was an avid conversation in progress Monday morning when Betty arrived to work. Mitch's wife was finally going to come home. The entire news's room crew sighed relief they'd all pulled together and cleaned the bosses' home and yard.

"When is her release scheduled? Will she still be wearing the cage? Is there going to be a nurse to accompany them?" A never-ending stream of questions kept surfacing, but no one was absolutely sure of the details.

Stela held up her fingers. "I'll phone and find out the exact details. We can meet briefly when everyone comes back to the office this afternoon. Cookie and Goldie were already planning the return party.

Steve didn't look at Betty, Gary or Leo. Instead he assigned Tiny and Tom the morning story that was developing. Gary listed with only half an ear; he was far more interested in his asking Betty out again and ways to monopolize more of her time. Leo figured as much.

Steve was alert to the surfacing situation. "He added,

"I've found out Todd is scheduled for release this week too."

The girls suppressed shudders with the ideas of two return parties to plan. After all it had been a busy year. The team raised their hands in high fives and left for their assignments.

As resigned as Steve felt, he was relieved Mr. Mosley was returning. His features were beginning to form a network of spider web wrinkles, radiated out from around his eyes and the corners of his mouth. The engulfing rush of news crowded him and the mad rush of others around him sent him into tailspins. Steve would feel relieved when the power button was finally turned off. He hadn't any desire to run a paper fulltime. He was still young and single, although he didn't mind the last three months of extra work. The end in sight left him feeling a little less frayed. Goldie's attention also captivated him.

Babbs's day was fully planned; she was meeting with several restaurateurs offering them a combined catering job for the council members and the upcoming Job Fair. Business as usual. In the back of her mind she knew her newfound duties would probably shift again with Todd's return to work. She'd miss the locals and the food. Her waistline wouldn't.

Stela, Goldie and Cookie would have been perfect entertainment schedulers. They seemed to balance everything into neat little packages on a stringed budget. Then there were all the other duties they had to man. Steve was really amazed at the work output.

Upon return later in the afternoon, they'd typed a

tentative list of what and when and how things would be timed. They even had assignments for the staff to bring what food, paper plates, napkins, and drinks and so forth for next Wednesday. It would be a busy week for all.

Gary knew what he wanted. Despite the loose ends he had to tie up with the paperwork at the office he'd made time to think about his approach with Betty. She was what he wanted. There were no other words he could find to express what she made him feel. How he felt about her and only her.

After work he popped on over to her place, barely knocking the door. He was bending over her now, and felt a little dizzy. With one shaky breath he seemed to give up on words. He had a one-hundred-kilowatt smile that would have made Simon the talent scout proud.

Sunlight slashed through the windows above the sink. Temperate air clogged in, smelled overpoweringly of her perfume, a citrus-flavored scent. Just beyond the kitchen, a sliding glass door was partly open and looking onto an enclosed back porch, floored in seasoned redwood and dominated by a table covered in lacy material a gray Manx stretched out sunning, watched him fearfully from up on the table, fur bristled.

She must have been anticipating his arrival he thought. Betty let Gary kiss her on the cheek, the edge of her ears, the corner of her lips, and sometime for a second she teased him with a lingering pause. Gary swore the sky had been cloudless since she arrived and even after the rain double rainbows had appeared. He had a wish; only half believing it might come true. She's finally going to tell him he was the only one and say yes to dating each other exclusively, become engaged, marry and have children, if she wanted. Above all just being happy.

Gary thought that when he died he'd go to heaven because he'd spent his time in hell without her. His jaw tightened, and he clamped his teeth together. He knew he couldn't answer questions left hanging, and sensed somehow it would be a mistake to prod her any faster. He was startled to find himself nodding in agreement with himself. Gary felt subtly cut off from his body, a witness, not a participant in the scene playing itself out. There was a pain in his gut, a sign of how deep his wound was.

The week sped by quickly and Wednesday fast approached. Mitch Mosley was sitting in his office that morning. It was if he'd never left.

All the girls noticed his hair appeared darker and luster shined his thinning head. He was even whistling, a tune they hadn't heard in quite a while.

Promptly at 9:00 a.m. he appeared in the news's room, collecting the staff. He expressed gratitude to the ones that tidied his home. His wife was relieved and settled comfortable with a nursing companion. His days would be short at first, but gradually over the next week his schedule would be back to normal. He noted how the office was running like a well-oiled machine, and how proud he'd been of each member of the Stanly Gazette team.

To their surprise a much thinner and handsome Todd walked in the side door. Everyone but Mitch was tackled off guard. They had developed a close friendship at the hospital. Both of their eyes were wide-open slits, showing signs of rest and relaxation. Betty guessed Todd had lost at least one third of his weight. The room brightened, surprise tugged at her heart. There was no sound for a moment, but the sudden whoosh of the closing office door. Everyone linked slowly, the tone was hopeful. A sensation of order and control flooded the room. A teardrop of happiness spilled from Babbs's eye. In the intensity of united spirits, the room became a photographic negative, all stark white and possibilities suspended in the moment. Time had skipped, but it didn't matter anymore.

Stela had found out and quickly changed the banner to include Todd in the welcome back party they'd hold at break.

Betty thought she must have taken an accelerated course in mind reading and admired how she was dressed.

Mitch announced the positions would shift back to their former workers. He pointed his index at Betty and asked to meet him in his office after the meeting. She was surprised, but knew this was to be expected. Taking a seat Mr. Mosley closed the door. "To you, Betty Babbs," he said. "This looks like the beginning of a brilliant career. Babbs, since you're the new hire and you've done a stupendous job, I've thought of a permanent position for you. Surprised her mouth opened and her penciled eyebrows lifted.

A slow smile crossed Mitch's face. "You'd make a perfect editor for the church news's section and miscellaneous activities about town. Of course, you'd be entitled to a salary increase and I hope you will accept my offer. You've turned out to be invaluable." He didn't add the part where her attractive self would be missed should she turn down the offer.

Betty was all smiles. "Yes!" She held her arms up in triumph. "Splendid!" She was swooning for a future she could build on. Noisy tears tried to slide down her cheeks, but she pushed them back.

In addition, she'd be supervisor to Stela, Goldie and Cookie. That in itself would be a full time job. But one she could handle. They'd become close friends.

20 — THE PANORAMA

Saturday had arrived as quickly as Leo. He approached her wearing a sleeveless V-neck t-shirt and she watched how the dimming sun reflected the silver of his crown. She was dressed simply, slacks and sandals and a light jacket. She wore earrings whose colors matched those in her necklace and bracelet. A backpack hung from her shoulder, and each time she moved her head, her hair swung freely. He kissed her cheek and hand as dark clouds hovered over the church planned fishing trip. Thank goodness it hadn't rained. She could see Leo's eyes fly toward her pupils that had calmed.

Although she embraced him warmly he sensed a change in her mood toward him. Betty seemed less desperate, less possessive, less concerned with her love life. Uncertainty circled him.

Babbs knew everyone was partial to her "Better Than Sex Cake" so she had baked one for the occasion. And she was infamous for hers, although nobody realized it was her recipe. The churchwomen leaned in, passed coat hangers and marshmallows full circle. The fire crackled. In this light Betty watched the full faces and happily drifted in and out of the moment. Gary had gone to the store to pick up more hot dog buns and Pepsi. She watched Leo sit back, extend his palms, stretch his arms over his head lean back, satisfied with the group he'd joined. He looked straight into Betty's eyes. His eyebrows raised, but his eyes told her he couldn't add anymore to the special moment. He stared at her as if she was a hot fudge sundae and he hadn't eaten for days.

The surprise was yet to come. One hand swooped his pocket, picked it, and a small box opened in front of her. A Tiffany box no less. When he pulled the lid back, a ring sparkled white gold and a single stone shined. It spilled from his hand to hers, catching her left ring finger and his question hung before her eyes in its entire splendor. A show-stopping moment and a showstopper diamond.

"Wow," the others echoed.

Betty's eyes sizzled like fireworks on a stick. Despite the way he'd caught her off guard she knew something wasn't right. She wasn't sweating, crying, heart racing, and knew immediately she wasn't ready for commitment. She felt as if she'd strung Leo along for attention like her last name lingered on other's tongues. Sure she had practiced Betty Babbs Sparks in verbiage, and on paper, but she'd also practiced Betty Babbs Leatherwood as well.

She watched him, her eyes brimming with tiny tears, at the scene he'd just made.

He glanced down and saw the look. "What?" he asked.

She tilted against him, her fingers tracing his jaw line.

"I was just counting my blessings," she said in a whisper. "It's impossible to believe, but I have too many." He bent and kissed her forehead with breathless tenderness. "As many as grains of sand in the ocean," he said throatily, with profound feeling, his dark eyes shimmered with it. "I'll cherish you all my life. All the way down into the dark. And the last picture I want in my mind is to be your face, smiling at me."

Tears dribbled down her cheeks. "I do love you, but I'm still young."

He wanted to kiss away her tears. "I'll never stop."

Somehow it was not quite what she wanted yet. She said, "There are no rules, you know? No rush?"

"But?" he whispered.

"So if we marry or if we don't, it will not change who we are or what we feel."

He nodded in agreement. She rubbed her head a little against the place where his neck joined her shoulder.

Stela, Goldie and Cookie all oohed and aahed, outlining the word Tiffany with their fingers on the box edge, feeling the light blue velvet bag. What it all added up to was a flash dance – happiness, hope, and security passed her way. She knew immediately what the answer was and pushed the ring back.

"It's too ceremonious right now," she answered. "You know we'd hate being married. Commitment is a serious issue."

Betty's actions were explosions of dreams inside her heart, and more than anything she didn't want to be wicked. Posed in a strapless striped dress, standing in a field of daisies, she'd thrown petals of love his way, but now she felt the need to hold him so tight he would hardly be able to breathe.

Leo looked shocked. His jaw dropped, appeared unglued and his face whitened. Everyone was watching, listening, not knowing what to say, leave or pretend nothing had happened. The onlookers drifted in other directions.

His face was entirely blank. Betty couldn't believe her own eyes or words. If his expression changed at all, it was because of a faraway look that came into his eyes, like he wasn't even listening to her, but had entered some state of acceptance all his own. She put her hand on his shoulder and even reached out to embrace him. But he pulled away as if stung by her touch. The pain in his heart was intense. His voice was strained, pitched to just above a whisper. When she glanced up at him, he was trembling, although his face was aglow with beaded sweat. His eyes glistened from deep in their dark and silent hollows. He couldn't think past it to line words up into clear sentences. The constriction was around his heart, a sickening tightness.

"Take care," they both said, at exactly the same time, in perfect unison. Leo squeezed her hand and nodded, but had nothing else to say. His heart was shaking with its wild, helpless throb. He couldn't even manage a comeback. Betty knew his heart was breaking as his face had gone deathly pale.

There were still churches she hadn't visited and men she hadn't met. She knew Leo was disappointed, and she excused herself from the party, dismissing herself due to a work issue that was past due. Anyway, why was everyone so concerned about her love life?

At the sight of Betty walking away, Leo felt an almost overwhelming throb of emotion: shock and loss and love all together. He could hardly bear to feel so much at once. Maybe it was more feeling than the reality exposed in the open could bear as well. His world had bent at the edges of his vision, life becoming blurred and distorted. The voices of the other girls on the beachfront deepened and dragged Leo to the point of incoherence. It was like listening to karaoke that slows down after the mike has been unplugged. Leo was on the verge of calling Betty back, wanted more than anything for her to turn back to him. He held himself back, stopped his racing heart and grasped the fragile situation at hand. It was important to remain quiet and to take no rash action. He tried to feel as little as possible and simply watched.

Goldie exclaimed, "God-awful! What are you nuts, Betty?"

"No," Betty stated, "I'm one of the sanest people I know. That's what makes this all so strange. Honestly, what's happening seems too crazy to talk about now."

Stela simply stated, "Life's too short."

And for Cookie her eyes sparkled with opportunity, feverish eyes, and immediately thwarted Leo's attention from an embarrassing moment, stating, "All of us wear masks, honey, crimson ones for anger, lacquered paper-mache for our demons, clear plastic molded ones to outline our face, and others that hang above each other – a lone black eye mask, silvery, glittery party masks, ones that only cover the eyes and a little of the nose. I think of it as taking a vacation from oneself. Why would anyone want to be the same person day in, day out? Our only decision is how we choose to receive the world. The secret to avoiding unhappy losses is to only play games you make up yourself." Her hips cut crescents toward him. She moved slowly, and then quicker, without losing the rhythm, and her arms tied bows around his air.

"We have a manageable problem," she quickly offered.

Leo's cheeks exploded the air and denial music whined on and on in the night. He felt lost in the wave of it, or maybe the depth. Cookie crossed her arms and clasped fingers around the hem of a tight t-shirt, lifted it to the sky and tossed it aside revealing her swimsuit and said, "Let's go for a swim."

Betty walked slowly away thinking; maybe, the town will sleep peacefully tonight. She's behind her wheel, humming a hymn to herself as she drives. She arches her back, stretches her spine, and keeps both hands on the wheel debating about church services on Sunday.

Leo would keep her in his memories, the mocking glance of her eyes, hair the color of honey and how she swayed like penciled pines caught in the rhythm of wind. But he also knew he wasn't going to give up this easy.

Gary would certainly be shocked when he returned to hear about the chain of events. Leo smiled. At least he beat him to the draw for once.

Mitch Mosley smiled secretly, as he pushed his handicapped wife toward the water where he planned to plant a big kiss on her. Mitch and his wife nodded solemn hellos. "Couple of characters there," Mitch spoke to his wife. "They might be us someday. If it is meant to be." Mosley finally knew the culprit that baked the best cake in the world as he had watched the arrival of each person. And so aptly named he thought. He would guard Betty's secret. He knew information was valuable. Especially when it was someone else's secret.

Even Todd had arrived with an extremely attractive woman, everyone still stupefied by his transformation. Babbs was thinking that actually, Wisenheimer, had acted like a hungry cat waiting to devour an overweight rodent, and even he had changed for the better. Speaking softly to herself, "Strange, what love can do?"

Babbs hadn't made any promises, or broken any promises. This occasion would probably be one of many curious pigeons would observe. The entire world gave off a delicate fragrance. After all life with her would never be passive, as she loved the feigned imaginations of others. A new diner had opened in Norwood and she felt like dessert.

She was even thinking ahead to invite Tiny for dinner and follow up by asking him to take her to the local VFW dance. A high voltage smile crossed her face. She might even display some scant cleavage via her Victoria Secret's push up bra. She knew by 11:00 p.m. she would be joined with other people becoming the life of the party, singing karaoke and shag dancing to beach music.

After all how can something be real – realer than real – if it just hangs there? You had to have your dreams. And her dream was to find a slim love-handled man, the kind with hard bones and a tendency to flee from time to time: something she called space. Her desire is to cast off old clothes, rise like a belly dancer's navel in seduction against the tasseled gray.

She thinks of Armageddon how the sun shatters, waves fragments one moment, glitters like jewels the next.

Antimatter obscures the sea of belief, opaque and flat, lead-colored; yet again, minutes later, the sun reemerges, strikes the waves scintillates nerve-like patterns, hypnotic to the eye, and how the planet revolves around everyone's head like a moon of pensive waters. Thick rainbow oil slicks ribbon the air, paint plasma color, whispers spell to birth foreknown future.

Betty's spirit moves like an echo travels in the distance and the sweet whispers of life to come beckons.

Betty Babbs thinks this is the stuff you send to be read in personal ad columns.

> *Happy girl looking for a change, please write. Need for a man maintaining a pedestal quality, able to wear tight fitting jeans with glacier cool, eyes that always dance in the company of others, willing to live next to train tracks, leaving past. Must pay rent money to share morning sounds, and a dog howling to be set free in alabaster light. The view - Crepe myrtles catch fire each spring, and the blackbird outside the window always sings.*

The part she couldn't write was: how she'd liked to pose in her red garters, hands on her thighs, wear her cat-shaped glasses, appearing higher than bridged crossing, squinting at sun, recently released from first stretch she'd known, or how she was used to dangerous men.

About the Author: Sarah Picklesimer Wilson

Sarah is a native Appalachian from North Carolina. Wilson enjoys all forms of writing, reading, painting, is an avid quilter, which evolves from her native roots. She lives with passion and sincerely hopes you enjoy reading her books.

"If we must part, Then let it be like this; Not heart on heart, Nor with the useless anguish of a kiss; But touch mine hand and say; "Until tomorrow or some other day, If we must part." "Words are so weak When love hath been so strong; Let silence speak; "Life is a little while, and love it long; A time to sow and reap, And after harvest a long time to sleep But words are weak."